ONCE UPON A GUY #1

THE**GUY** WITH THE**SUITCASE**

CHRIS ETHAN

To Tracy.

Enjoy.

Hugs -

Chris

Copyright © 2016 by Rhys Christopher Ethan

Published by Dream Trek Imprint

Cover Design by
Ethereal Ealain
(etherealealain.com)

Edited by
Kameron Mitchell
& Jules Robin

visit Chris Ethan's website at:
rcethan.com/chris

Chapter 1
Pierce

What do you mean, yes, if I suck your dick?"

"What ya heard, kiddo. Yes, I might have a bed for ya, if ya suck my dick," the guy said. The cluttered desk he was seated at as disheveled as Pierce himself.

"How—?" Pierce was struggling to find the right words and express his emotions rather than punch his way to a bed and a shelter for the night. He sucked in a deep breath and tried again. "I need a bed, dude. I'm homeless; you're a homeless shelter. Help a dude out," he said, on his best behavior. He hadn't done that in a while. That was one of the benefits of living on the streets. No one gave a shit about you, and unless you were harassing someone, no one gave a shit if you had a fit.

Waiting for the charity worker's reply was as nerve-wracking as waiting for a reply from one of his college applications, just two years before. The man glanced both ways as he'd done before, giving a quick check around him, even though they were in a small room, no bigger than two-by-two and with no chance of anyone overhearing him.

"I know, dimwit, I heard ya the first time. And what I said is help a brother out, and he'll help ya back," he said in a sly, infuriating tone, as if his whole life depended on that blowjob.

Pierce winced. "You are a charity worker, right? You're supposed to help me no matter what. Not asking for oral, which between the two of us is really unethical," he admonished, shifting from one leg to the other, making a real effort to not lose it and fuck up his chances of getting a corner in this crowded and smelly New York shelter. The silence in between their conversation was dressed with snores and some manic wails in the far distance.

The guy shrugged. "A guy's got needs. Ya know what I'm talking about. Was talking to this guy on Grindr and suddenly my power died, leaving me all horny," he explained with a nonchalance that was not befitting to the place.

"You know what?" Pierce had heard enough. That was the last straw. "Go and fuck yourself, you asshat. I'd rather sleep another night on the streets than suck your toothpick," he spat. He picked up his old, leather suitcase that was waiting for him on the floor.

"Fuck you, bastard. I'll be damned if ya ever get a bed in here," the guy shouted at him as Pierce ducked outside, ready for some silence after such an upsetting encounter.

That was the problem with people. They could be real assholes when they started talking, so he preferred it when they didn't. Best example? His own parents. Had they not spoken, had he not told them he was gay, they wouldn't have kicked him out. He would still have a family. But people had to talk and ruin everything. Even himself. So he rather preferred to stay silent—when the monster inside of him wasn't scratching to be released and wreak havoc at idiots like that pervert.

He tightened his fist around his suitcase handle and forced one foot in front of the other, pushing through the exhaustion and the numbness in his toes, a side effect of the imminent winter in New York City. He'd need a coat to survive it. A coat and a sleeping bag, among other warm things. He needed to find some but wasn't sure were to look. If he had to, he was could steal them. Anything to survive that fucking winter.

His feet somehow led him to Central Park—perhaps habit, perhaps it was really just around the corner. He didn't know, and he no longer cared. He just wanted to find a safe spot and close his eyes for as long as possible. He needed to rest. He hadn't slept in four days.

The breeze rustling through the leaves gave him a cool welcome back to old haunts, and he quickly found a bench, solitary in existence, perfectly matching its new owner. He lay flat on it and trying to think warm thoughts. He put the suitcase under his head to keep it safe and shut his eyes for the first time in forever.

His face felt steaming hot, and liquid ran down his nose and wet his eyebrows. Was it raining? He was sure it wasn't. He would have felt his whole body drenched in water. No. This was something else. He opened his eyes to find them stung by the toxicity of piss. Three guys wearing hoodies and smug expressions on their faces all had their dicks out, pointed at Pierce, and were relieving themselves on his sleepy face.

He sprang up and pushed one of them back. "What the fuck, man?"

The thugs laughed.

"Look, the junkie is alive. Bro, we were worried you had flatlined," the guy he had pushed said.

"Are you serious? What the actual fuck? What is wrong with you?" he shouted as he wiped the piss off his face with the sleeve of his pullover.

"Look, man, we thought you overdosed or something. We were trynna wake yo' ass," another guy said and giggled like the sorry little girl he was soon going to be.

Pierce glared at him. "Overdose? Me? That looks more like your territory, fuckwit," he replied.

"Hey, man, chill. Why you usin' that language? We didn't offend you," said the third guy, playing it cool.

"You fucking pissed on me. That I take as a fucking offense, you asshole," Pierce shrieked.

The laughter fell off the guy's face and he assumed an offensive stance. He shoved Pierce backward onto the bench. His palm came into contact with the same mix of urine that was drenching his face. Big fucking mistake.

Pierce growled from between his teeth. "You're going to regret that, dick." Pierce kicked the guy's groin, making him shudder and drop his upper body forward. Pierce pushed his foot on the guy's face, and he flew back onto the ground. Pierce stood up again and raised his fists at the other two guys, ready to defend himself.

"Have I made myself clear yet?" he

huffed, the anger in him still burning for some action.

He was disappointed as the perpetrators all ran off into the darkness without another word. Pierce grabbed his suitcase. It was drenched like him, and he cursed the skies for his shitty luck tonight. What more could possibly go wrong? So many months on the streets, and he had hardly experienced as bad a night as tonight's.

He found the closest spigot, took his sweater off and put it to the side, his nipples hardening at the biting cold and the hairs on his arms raising to ward it off. He washed his face and hair, the ice cold water making him breathless and numb. That was it. He was going to die of frostbite because a bunch of idiots decided his face looked like a toilet.

He growled. He hated this. He hated not having a house anymore. Not having his own space. He didn't appreciate how important home was when he had it. Now all he could do was hope he didn't die overnight, sleeping on benches, subways, and tarmacs.

When he felt adequately clean, he grabbed his sweater and gave it a good soak. He was going to have to wait for it to dry, a hopeless pursuit already. He opened his small suitcase and pulled a t-shirt out. A jet black T-shirt he had been wearing back in the summer when his parents kicked him out. He pulled it on. This was going to be a stupid night.

Chapter 2
Rafe

afe walked past the busy streets of Times Square feeling breathless and unhinged. He hated begging at the horrible place, but every dime counted in his situation. It wasn't enough, however. A count of the change in his hand told him so. It was never enough. It was only a supplement to make up for the hot cocoas he bought during the day. He always had to go north at the end of each day and make more.

Not everyone who occupied the streets of this crowded town chose to make money that way, but then again not every one of them had the effect a skinny Latino boy had on older men.

Some were ugly old fucks, reeking of alcohol, too lost in their addiction to do anything about it, only beg for more booze. Some were too proud to sleep with people for shelter and cash. Some were just hypocrites, begging in rags during the day and being driven around town in limos in the evening.

Rafe had seen them all, met them all. Besides the fake ones, there were three kinds of homeless people in New York City: the old junkies, the new junkies, and the faggots. Rafe was lucky to only belong in the last category. He wasn't going to put anything in his body to make him a dead man walking; he was hopeless enough as it was. His *madre* needed him and he wasn't going to let her down by dying at twenty. Not if he could help it.

Oh, how he missed her. He hadn't seen her in months, but he had heard her voice almost daily. He would call her every day at 4 p.m., when he knew she would be at home and his *padre* still at work. He never spoke to her, just listened to her voice answering the phone.

Thinking of his *madre* and trying to escape the hectic streets, if only for a while, had brought him to a side of Central Park where a young man was washing a piece of clothing. He looked annoyed, straining his sweater over a spigot of running water and mumbling something between his teeth. His torso was exposed to the cool night. He was fit. His muscles were as thick as both Rafe's arms together, and his chest pumped full with veins. His ribs were a swoon-worthy sight. His hair was dark, but wherever the light touched it appeared ginger.

He noticed a small, rectangular leather suitcase. Brown and covered in stickers faded from wear. What was a homeless man doing with a vintage suitcase like that in the middle of Central Park? Had he stolen the bag? And if he had, what did the bag hold that was so important? Perhaps it contained money, the money Rafe needed to survive. If it was stolen already, then stealing it himself wouldn't hurt anyone.

He watched as the man grabbed a black T-shirt from the ground next to the suitcase and pulled it on. Rafe found his opportunity. His feet initiated the run before he could stop himself and think twice. In all the months that he had been homeless, he had never stolen something of value. Until now.

While the man was still busy putting on the tee, Rafe grabbed the suitcase handle and sped away from the spigot. The darkness of the park gave him cover, but he continued to run through pathways and past trees until he felt safe enough to stop. He put the suitcase down and flipped the clasps open. Before he had a chance to lift the flap and sneak a peek at what was inside, though, he felt the sting of pain in between his shoulder blades and collapsed on the ground next to the bag, gasping for breath.

The owner of the suitcase appeared in front of him with a swift kick to the stomach.

"You stupid motherfucker. I've had enough for one night. You got me? Take your disgusting hands away from my stuff," he said and lifted his foot, preparing a second attack. Rafe turned to face him and put his hands between himself and the man.

"Sorry, dude. I really need the money," he said with a single breath.

The man picked his suitcase and kicked Rafe's knees lightly. "And I don't? Do I look like I'm the fucking Queen of England?" he growled and swore incoherently.

"I'm sorry, okay? I don't know what else to say. Just…" Rafe took a deep breath, swallowing the pain in before he continued, "just stop beating me, okay?"

The man looked down at him, inspected his face and then spat on the ground next to him.

"Fuck you," he grumbled and walked away, leaving Rafe utterly humiliated, lying on the ground, assessing his sores and his would-be bruises. The sounds of the city drowned as he came to the realization of what he'd just done.

"*Éstupido*," he said to himself, slapping the tarmac under him. He wasn't so much upset that he'd attempted to steal a suitcase but that he'd gotten caught and beaten for it.

He decided to stop feeling sorry for himself and continue his journey. He got up, dusted his pride off, and marched out of the park and up to Harlem, following Manhattan Avenue up to Morningside Park. A little over 110th was his usual spot.

He reached the dimly lit street where a couple of black boys were bending their miniature bodies to accentuate their best features and get one of the good businessmen to spend their Hamiltons and Jacksons on their asses. Rafe never had to do anything of the sorts. He just had to lean back on one of the cars and talk to the drivers. What most of them rentboys didn't understand yet was that these guys were everyday people, perhaps lonely, perhaps shy or not confident enough in their skin, who still wanted to feel the carnal pleasures of sex. They weren't billionaires who wanted a boy toy. Rafe had quickly picked that up. He was a smart guy, perhaps not science-worthy or an excellent mathematician, but he had street smarts, a much-needed skill if you were homeless.

In addition to his smarts, Rafe was a naturally charming kid. He was skinny, yes, but also relatively short, so his lack of weight didn't look unnatural. He had a good round butt that was visible through any clothing he wore, and he tried to change outfits at least once a week, buying from thrift stores and discarding his old clothes. He didn't have a lot of muscle anywhere else but his butt, but his skin was smooth like milk chocolate and his hair was trimmed military short. His eyebrows were black and thick and he loved that feature on his face. It added a touch of masculinity to his rather effeminate appearance.

But his hands? His hands did all the work whenever a guy was considering picking him up. They had never failed him. He had never been ditched for someone else. His hands were all over the guy before he had even decided. He would rub the driver's window until the guy put his elbow out at which point he would guide his hand up and down their shoulder, gently, softly, fingers dancing ethereally and no matter if they wore a T-shirt or a suit, none could resist the feelings the delicate action awoke in them.

Rafe left his 'competition' to their business, and he relaxed against a van parked at the street. He rubbed his scalp and, taking a deep breath, felt the soreness on his back from where the guy had hit him. He hoped it wouldn't get in the way of his job. He was about to find out, as a car stopped in front of him. Rafe had deducted that as soon as he relaxed, work would find him. He had also decided to add a tiny bit of sensuality to his movements and bam! He was in business. It worked every time.

When the car window rolled down, Rafe got to work. It was getting too cold to be sleeping in Central Park and getting beaten by handsome homeless guys.

Chapter 3
Pierce

The chill of early morning tugged Pierce's limp body, waking him up before the sun's rays did. He rubbed his eyes with dead cold fingers. It felt invigorating on his sleepy face. Much preferable to washing it with ice water. He rested his palm on his eyes and let it refresh them in what little way it could. It almost felt welcoming.

Cold was stupid like that. It could send you to shivers, making you think you were gonna die of it, but once you got used to it, it was almost comfortable. Almost being the key word.

His body was stiff. He decided to stretch his

muscles and revitalize his bones by doing a little jog around the park before the commute started in the busy streets of New York. He walked down 7th and squatted at Times Square subway station. He took a small piece of cardboard out of his suitcase and held it next to him as he waited for people's generosity to strike.

Sure enough, in a matter of few minutes, suits and arrogance hit the streets as everyone had to be somewhere, anywhere but the streets, which somehow never seemed to empty, not even after dark. But of course that was something to be expected in the city that never sleeps. He earned nothing from the office people who didn't have enough time to waste on a lower being like Pierce.

But soon the tourists descended, filling the square with all the cultural clichés that one could possibly find in one place. And naturally, the mascots that everyone loved to hate appeared, looking to cash in on another day's work.

Pierce was jealous. He was jealous of everyone that had a job, a place to be. An occupation that gave you a purpose—or a sense of it, anyway. Sure, being a waiter for all his life wasn't his idea of a good life. He had worked on campus when he was still in college and had grown accustomed to the hopelessness that ensued with a job of that calibre, but he would exchange that hopelessness for the one lingering inside of him every day he spent waking up without purpose.

Reminiscing about a life once comfortable was such a pastime sitting there on the pavement, waiting for people's charity, that he didn't notice when a kid started staring at him, tugging his mom's hand to draw their attention to him.

"Mommy, can we help this boy? He's got no home," he said.

The mother turned and at first seemed dumbfounded as to why her son found Pierce so interesting, but then her eyes trailed to the sign next to him: *My family kicked me out for being gay. Now I have no home. Please help me get back on my feet.*

Her eyes hardened as she reached the end, and then she looked at her son, a boy probably of eleven years, dressed in pink converse and large clothes on his petite frame.

"Sure we can, sweetie." She reached for her bag just as the apparent father caught up with his family. He asked them what they were doing.

There it was. Pierce was certain, now the father was there, they would all walk away, intimidated by the patriarch's refusal to help a homeless fag. He'd seen that look a few times. A macho, big guy with dark features and even grimmer expression shooing people away from the sinner. This dad fit the profile.

Having all that in his mind, Pierce didn't say anything to them, waiting for the outcome. He was shocked when the father leaned in and said in the kindest voice he had ever heard come out of a man his size, "You okay, fella? Can I get you something to eat?"

Pierce couldn't believe he was awake. He had nothing to say. All words had abandoned his brain. He only managed to nod and watch as the guy walked to the nearest food stand. He came back and handed him a couple of paper boats full of food. Pierce took them in his hands, replying with a quiet thanks. And just as he thought they were done with him, the woman knelt down and passed him a few bills, squeezing his hand tight.

"Here. Get yourself a hostel for the night. I wish I could do more," she whispered to him, eyes trailing towards where her son stood behind her.

"You can," he told her and her eyes widened at his response. "You love your son?" She nodded. "Make sure he knows it," he finished, throwing a glance at the boy.

The mother's eyes reddened before she gave his hand another gentle squeeze and got up, resuming their journey.

He stayed in Times Square for a few more hours, saving the second boat of food for when his hunger hit him again. He loathed the taste of meat on his palate, but being homeless, he couldn't accommodate his veganism when he didn't know when his next meal would be or whom it would come from. He had done that the first few days of being homeless when people offered to buy him some food, and they would eye him warily when he appeared picky or resistant to accepting a burger.

Another thing about living on the streets was that hunger was a constant enemy he had to battle. Sure, the first few weeks were hard to get used to, when his body was constantly complaining about not being fed every three hours like he used to do when he was in college. Slowly, his stomach got accustomed to a meal a day and learned to appreciate it for what it was. That didn't, however, mean that the brain ever stopped craving and reminding him what he was missing out on. As if it wasn't enough that the food odors coming from all sorts of restaurants could make his mouth salivate, his mind would make him lose awareness of his surroundings in order to introduce another imaginary dish into his fantasy.

Some more people stopped to give him some change. He had found out that if people saw him with food while he was begging, they were more likely to stop and give him their quarters. Not if he was eating, though. That seemed to have a worse result than if he was shooting heroin up his arm. He guessed people liked to see a beggar buy food with his money, but if they saw him eat, they thought he didn't need any more and might spend whatever they spared on drugs.

That was yet another thing about being homeless. People constantly assumed he did drugs. It didn't matter if his eyes were white and clear or if he wore T-shirts with unpunctured skin, the homeless-drug-use correlation affected everyone. Which was why he would curse every time he saw one of his 'homies' do illegal substances in front of the public. They were ruining everyone's chances of getting some money. Sure, some did drugs or ended up doing them to survive the mental demons that crept up in them when living on the streets, but there were some like Pierce who didn't have any affiliation to any drug of any form. Before he'd been left to die on the streets, he'd been studying nutrition and fitness. He'd actually kill himself before he touched those horrible, mind-numbing things.

When the sun began to set behind the city skyscrapers, Pierce decided to call it quits for the day and make his way to a hostel. He was thankful that he'd be avoiding enraging homeless shelters, pissing thugs, suitcase thieves, and the motherfucking cold for one night. Hopefully, the money could buy him two nights. He hadn't even counted the notes the mother had given him. He'd stuffed it in his pants. He didn't want to be seen counting notes while begging. No one would give him a buck.

He was glad to find out he had made twenty bucks from all the change and bills he'd been tossed. And even more excited to find he had fifty from the mother. Seventy dollars surely could buy him a couple of nights at the hostel. He was over the moon.

He made his way up to 116th where a few two-star hostels were situated around the block. He'd tried a couple whenever he'd made enough, but they were all very wary about hosting a homeless man, even though Pierce didn't look it.

He had gone to a lot of effort to not appear homeless. He did want people's compassion and their change when he was begging, which is why he would find a cardboard to lay on when he did, but he would discard it as soon as he'd finished for the day and go on a quest to find a roof for the night. He wasn't a hoarder. He'd seen those people countless times, carrying all the crap they could find and the way passersby would eye them. He didn't want that. He wanted to be treated like any other person. How else would he fight the situation he was in? No, for him, his suitcase was enough. Maybe he smelled a little, especially on days when he hadn't found a shelter for a few nights, but he always recuperated once he had. Tonight was gonna be such a night.

He decided not to visit one of those hostels he had used before. He took a turn around a few blocks and came to one place he had seen before and passed by but had never actually stayed in. It was very close to a donut shop and a clothing store, both of which could turn out useful the next morning, depending on how much the hostel was charging. Honestly, he wouldn't mind sleeping there only a night if it meant he could buy a coat for the winter and have a good shower. Or a bath even, if they had one. And of course some laundry couldn't hurt.

He lingered outside for a while, not sure about going in. It always happened to him. Whenever he made enough for a hostel, he always contemplated saving the money for something else. Like the coat he so desperately needed, or heavier clothes, or boots. Or simply putting it inside his suitcase and saving it for food or saving it to rent a proper room in a proper apartment. But the former would only make him greedier with his daily meals, and the latter would only happen in a year or so and only if he managed to get a job. As hopeless as these choices sounded, he always considered them before spending his money.

A drop fell on his nose, sending shivers down his spine. It was going to rain. He couldn't sleep outside, and the subway would be full of his people on a rainy night. No. He shook his head and let himself in. It turned out the hostel was only charging twenty-five dollars a night, including the tax, and had a bed in a two-bedroom dorm.

That had never happened to him before. He usually had to sleep in a room with eight, twelve, sixteen people, often clutching his suitcase so tight during the night that he'd wake up with a numb arm.

He booked two nights and decided to keep the rest for sustenance. The girl behind the reception passed him the key to the dorm, and he took the elevator to the second floor.

As soon as he walked out into the corridor, he knew why it had been so cheap. The hostel was part of a block of flats, the hostel itself owning a few rooms of the entire floor. All the dorms' doors were colored light blue, like the company's logo. There were a few doors marked as either Restroom or Shower, and after a quick investigation, Pierce came to the conclusion that they were used by tenants and lodgers alike. Not a very welcoming fact, but it was better than nothing.

He found his room number and unlocked the room. There was no one inside. The lights were out, both beds plainly, if not terribly, dressed. Pierce flipped the switch and hid his suitcase under the bunk bed, placing his t-shirt on the bottom mattress to mark its occupancy. He held the keys in his hands and left the room to find a shower. When he found one, he locked the door and took off his shoes. His once white socks now screamed with dirt. He bent to take them off, simultaneously looking at the shower. The head was a single pipe protruding from the wall, covered in moss, and the floor was not in any better of a condition. A couple of bottles of shower gels were thrown on the ground. Having sufficiently undressed, he inspected their contents. They were almost empty but both had enough for one shower.

Score!

Both were shower gels, but he used one, the better smelling to wash his hair. The other one to lather up his body without the aid of a loofa.

Once he felt decently washed and finally rid of the stench of piss that'd been following him around since the previous day's incident, he wiped his body with his trousers, the cleanest of his clothes, and let his hair dry up naturally. He returned to his room, piled up all his clothes, and walked around the corridors in his underwear, looking for the laundry room. Of course there were none on this floor, so he called the elevator and rode it down to the basement.

He needed only a few quarters and to let his clothes run the cycle. He returned to his room; he was finally able to relax. Until he had to go back down to take his clothes back, but that wouldn't be for another couple hours. He spread out naked on the mattress and pulled his suitcase from under his bed. He placed it on his lap and flipped it open.

Everything he owned was in that bag. The money he had made today was there. A couple of packets of chips that he'd bought while contemplating the hostel. And the photographs.

He took the pile in his hands and browsed through them for the millionth time. Photographs from all over the world: Paris, London, Berlin, Mexico, Peru, Toronto, Melbourne, Sydney, Cape Town, Beijing, Tokyo. Pictures he wished he could live in rather than in this horrible reality that he had to tolerate. The photographs, faded as they were, brought a smile to his face, a flutter to his heart, and a burden to his stomach. They always made him feel so bittersweet.

Chapter 4
Rafe

afe left his latest patron's apartment complex and wrapped his jacket tightly around himself. He browsed around him, trying to locate a phone booth, but none were around. It was too early, anyway.

He really needed to hear his *mamá's* voice that instant, but she was still at work. He tried to shut his brain off and go about his usual business, trying to put the demons in their place. He always felt so confident being picked up, driven around to be fucked senseless wherever the customer found desirable. Until of course he actually let the men put their hands on him and use him as they wanted, as they found pleasurable, as they found payable.

The money he received at the end of each transaction only gave him half his dignity back. He left the other half behind him as he left the customers. Little by little, one would think, he'd have no dignity left, but it always managed to surprise him.

But that was his only way of making any sort of income. If he was gonna save money to buy his meds and get off the streets, it took a sacrifice. So what if he sacrificed his soul and all he was in the process? He was a good rentboy, but it didn't mean he enjoyed it one bit. He knew how to lure and seduce, how to please and satisfy, but it didn't mean he enjoyed sharing sweat and fluids with strangers. It was his life now, however. He wasn't proud of it, but then again what homeless guy was?

He walked around the streets and found a cafeteria to sit down and gulp some coffee. There was another challenge for him being a street man. What did he do between the last night and the next, after he'd fucked or been fucked and slept the night in a wet and warm bed? He always got coffee, but the after was always an unknown factor. A factor that changed. All he had to look forward to was the phone call to *madre*.

Sipping on a coffee with a few caramel drops, he made up his mind. He grabbed his rucksack and set off down for Queens, caught the bus, and got off as soon as he'd reached his destination. He'd been meaning to visit but always cowered. Today he had the balls to find the Social Services Center and walk into it.

"Hello, how can I help you?" a cheery woman asked him at the reception.

"Hi…um, I'd like to…uh…sign up for Medicaid?" he said with uncertainty in his voice.

"You need to go on the second floor and ask the reception for registration forms," she replied without missing a beat and pointed to the elevator.

He nodded a thanks and followed her directions, finding himself on the second floor. He saw a desk marked as Administration and approached the woman behind it, a much older lady with thick glasses, loose hair, and a leathery skin. She wore a fuchsia turtleneck and a beaded cross necklace around it.

"Hi, can I have the registration form for Medicaid?" he inquired.

The woman lifted her eyes and inspected him as if she was trying to put a name to the face. Rafe could have sworn he had never seen her before. After a few, uncomfortable seconds, she spoke, her eyes still small slits staring him up and down.

"Uh-huh." She nodded. With some

difficulty, she took her eyes off him and opened a drawer under her desk to pull a pile of sheets from inside it. "Here you go. You need to fill that in. There's a lot that you need to include on that registration. Once you're done, bring it back to me with a birth certificate, social security number, proof of address, and the last four weeks of pay stubs," she told him in a screechy voice that could make Rafe slap her senseless. It was that annoying. As was what she was telling him.

Pay stubs? Proof of address? He didn't have a second pair of socks, let alone a proof of address. It seemed as if his reluctance to visit the center wasn't so stupid after all. He'd just have to sleep with a few more clients, maybe raise his fee a little bit, and buy his own medication and make it last for as long as possible. How was he supposed to make one-a-day pills last six months on a one month prescription without killing himself?

The woman coughed and shook her hand that held the papers. Rafe took them from her and dropped them in his rucksack, making his way back out into the streets. What now? Where was he supposed to go? He looked at the time. It was three p.m. and he was only a few blocks from his house. It'd been a while since he'd done it, but he decided to take a walk by his old neighborhood. Catching a glimpse of his *madre* would probably suffice instead of calling her. She was going to get back from work any moment now.

He crossed the street and went into the next right. He saw her getting off a bus, not too far from their address at Forty-Six. She walked down the road with her bag in hand and her skirt flowing as she took the steps.

Mamá.

He hadn't seen her in so long that she looked older, stranger. As if she *was* a stranger. But he'd missed her arms and her soothing voice. He'd missed her food and her singing. He wanted to catch up with her, talk to her, but he couldn't. So instead he imagined what he'd say to her if he could.

She unlocked the front door, and before disappearing behind it, she turned. She looked around, inspecting the street. Her eyes trailed over Rafe, staring from afar, and he ducked behind a wall so that she wouldn't see him, his heart racing. He waited a minute, then looked back. His *madre* was still there, looking at where he was. She waved at him, and his heart plummeted. She knew it was him. She was looking for him. She missed him. But going to her would be risky. Fighting down the tears that were pushing through his eyes, he turned his back to her and walked away hastily, unwilling to acknowledge her. He just hoped she knew he did it for her. She was a smart woman. He hoped she knew. He crossed himself, praying to *María Guadalupe* to keep her safe.

He decided to take the subway and ride back to Manhattan. He had to make it out for her. He just didn't know how.

He found his way back to Times Square and headed south. Mario's Pizza was only a couple of blocks around the corner. It wasn't particularly busy, but it had been open for over forty years, so Rafe's guess was they made enough to stay open, and despite their lack of a constant stream of business, they offered Rafe and a few other homeless kids food for free. Especially Latinos. They had a pay-it-forward jar for customers, and instead of taking tips, patrons would leave a couple dollars for those who came in and were short of change or simply had none at all. The majority of the pay-it-forward service was used by the homeless of the area. Rafe was one of them. Marissa was another, a friend of his. They always met at four for late lunch at Mario's before Rafe would go out to call *madre*. Today that would not be necessary. He had seen her and she had seen him. It was more than he could ask for at the moment.

The good thing with Mario's, besides being able to eat free without begging to make enough for a slice, was that they could actually sit inside, get warm, enjoy a slice or two, and have some coffee to warm them up before venturing back into the wilderness of NYC.

Marissa was there when he entered the place. She was hard to miss. A naturally big girl with straight, jet black hair caught back in a ponytail, and black clothes —as per usual, a goth at the best of times. Her eyes were always smudged with some eyeliner she had managed to pocket from a beauty store. Her skin was much darker than Rafe's and her face was spotty, as with most teenagers.

She was a lesbian, and her parents had abused her since she'd come out to them at age sixteen. She ran away a year later after they'd beaten her senseless, calling her all sorts of names. She still had a scar under her left eye that was staying there for good. Rafe couldn't help but feel affection for the young girl and see her as his little sister, albeit being bigger than him, so he saw their daily meetings as a ritual. As a family gathering.

"Hey, *chica*, whassup?" he took a seat across her. She was holding a cup of tea, the steam rising up well above both of them.

"Hey," she said in an unusually miserable tone. That worried Rafe. She was always vocal and sassy, just like he liked her. She would always greet him with "Hey, guuurl!" and then high-five him. That didn't happen either.

"What's wrong, *chica*?" he asked her.

She breathed in and exhaled, changing the steam direction with her breath. "I bumped into my mother today," she huffed.

"What? How? Where?" He jumped in surprise, just as Mario's wife placed his hot cocoa on his side of the table.

"Union Square. She was out shopping with her girlfriends," she replied.

He cursed. It was one thing bumping across your godforsaken relatives in your neighborhood, but stumbling upon them in Manhattan was like finding the needle in the haystack. "What happened?"

"She took a good look at me, called me a slut, and cold-shouldered me. Even her girlfriends, the women I grew up around, wouldn't acknowledge me. God, I hate her so much, Rafe," she said and punched the top of the table, spilling a little of her tea and Rafe's cocoa.

He reached across the table and gave her his hand. "Fuck her, *chica*. She's no mother. Just fuck her and the lame excuse of a dad you have," he offered her. She took it with appreciation, bringing a slight smile on her face.

"So...what are we having today?" he continued, leaving the miseries of reality to the back of their minds and enjoying a good meal before returning to it.

"I'm having a Hawaiian," Marissa said. Rafe angled his head in surprise.

"Excellent choice, *señorita*. A Hawaiian for my *chica* and a pepperoni for me, please, Sonia," he called to Mario's wife, who was counting money at the register.

"One or two?" she asked without raising her eyes from the bills.

Rafe looked to Marissa who showed him two fingers, as usual. "Two, *por favor*," he told Sonia.

"Right away, *chico*," Sonia responded, closing the register and getting to work.

Marissa sipped her tea and set it back down, changing the subject. "What did you do today?"

"*Joder*! I went to get the Medicaid form. If I had all the things they ask for," he said through his teeth, "I wouldn't be applying for it, that's all I'm going to say, *chica*."

Marissa grimaced. "It's going to be okay, Rafe. We'll find a way."

He shook his head. "How, *chica*? I make, what? Fifty dollars a night, maybe? I've been saving for two months and I still can't afford the damn medicine. I'm getting worse, you know. I don't feel the energy I used to have. Even some of my clients have noticed. You know, the couple regulars that I fuck every week," he said.

"Well...how much have you got so far?" she asked. Sonia placed two slices in front of each of them.

"Fifteen hundred. I'm nearly there, but I keep thinking I'm gonna die before I get to the nineteen hundred that I need," he replied and started munching on his meal.

"That's eight more fucks or something, right? Can't you pick up anyone during the day?"

The stare that Rafe gave answered her question.

"I'm just asking. How the hell am I supposed to know how it works?"

"Trust me, *chica*, sometimes even *I* don't know how it works," he said, then resumed his eating.

When they both finished and enjoyed a second cup of hot drinks, they parted their ways, and Marissa went to the shelter she had been accepted in for the week.

Rafe had tried them all, was sick of them. They'd kick him out on the third night without notice or ask him to pay for a shower or a clean towel or simply claim they were full and send him off.

Rafe decided to test Marissa's suggestion and made his way to his pickup spot early, on the off-chance that guys might drive by, trying to pick someone up. As he suspected, as long as the sun was out, no traffic of his sort was available. And even deeper into the evening, nothing was moving. Around eight other boys began to assemble. There were about ten of them spread across the street in groups of two or three, all chatting, waiting for business to pick up.

Rafe was not friendly with any of them. He found other rentboys and their stories boring as fuck, and he'd be damned before he let himself be subjected to another stupid confession of what brought them to the specific profession. And even if their stories weren't all bullshit, he just couldn't stand them. All he wanted was to be picked up and make money, and that's what he'd do tonight again.

By nine, a couple were picked up by some early birds, but there was a stillness again until ten, when more cars started driving by. There were a few sixty-year-olds, one younger guy, and one car with two young guys, who looked like college students looking to have some fun if the guys they picked were any indication.

One by one—or in that instance, two by two—the street started to clear out, leaving Rafe dry. None of his regulars were here tonight. He would normally stay until two a.m., if he wasn't picked up straight away, which he normally did. But he'd been there since six and was starting to feel cold, despite the relatively friendly temperature that evening.

"Fuck it," he spat, resolving to spend his money on a hostel. He simply wouldn't have it today. He was very tight with his money, but today had been particularly disappointing. He'd been afraid to visit the council for weeks to pick up a Medicaid form, but when he was on his way there, he had dreamed it would be easy.

Well, that dream was crushed, and he was gonna treat himself to a bed without male companion beside him.

He walked uptown where he knew a cheap hostel, one that almost always had spare beds available last minute. He got the key in no time after he paid for the night and got the elevator to the second floor. He found the number easily.

When he entered the room, he jumped; a man was lying on the lower bunk, wearing only a pair of faded blue boxers, otherwise uncovered.

He was a steaming sight, specifically his crotch, bulky and surrounded by smooth white skin. The v-shape that led to the guy's dick was so lickable, he momentarily fantasized doing just that.

"Oh, fuck you," the guy exclaimed,

waking Rafe from his daze.

The guy came into view from under the bed as he stood up and put something in a brown leather suitcase. That suitcase was familiar.

It was *it*. It was *him*. The guy from yesterday. The *gilipollas* that had beaten him up.

"What are you doing here? Having an encore of last night's stupidity?" the guy said, holding the suitcase.

"No. Do you always hold the suitcase like it's an extension of your arm?" Rafe replied with a tiny bit of bile.

The guy gave him the finger and tucked his suitcase under the bed. "Don't even get into any ideas tonight," he told Rafe.

Rafe grimaced. Pierce was right. Rafe had tried to steal his suitcase and Pierce was justified for acting the way he had last night and the way he was talking to him now.

"I won't. Um…" He wanted to apologize but couldn't find the guts to. He paused. He swallowed his pride, like his *mamá* had taught him. "I'm sorry. I don't know what came over me," he said dropping his head to his chest.

"Greed?" the guy suggested.

Rafe eyed him and shrugged. "I guess," he said.

The guy rolled back onto the bottom bunk and stretched out his body. The sight was once again irresistible to Rafe, but he restrained himself as he made his way to the bed and threw his rucksack on the top bunk.

"Do you always lie around in hostels in your underwear?" he asked him, unable to hold himself back any longer.

"My clothes are in the washing machine. I'm waiting for the cycle to finish," Pierce said, less aggressive now.

Rafe backed up to look at the guy clearer. "Wait! You went around the corridors like that? You must be very confident in your skin." Not that he had any reason not to be.

"I must be very homeless," he grunted.

Rafe laughed. He nodded in acknowledgement. "How did it happen for you?"

The guy picked up a book and turned his back to Rafe, murmuring, "It's none of your business."

"Fair enough," he replied. This guy was a fucking rock. No emotions, no feelings, just pure aggression. "I'm Rafe, by the way," he offered, hoping to break the ice.

The guy glowered at Rafe and put the book down. "Pierce," he growled.

Finally, Rafe was able to put a name on that chunk of man-candy that had given him a good beating. Pierce. Well, with such stunning eyes, it fit.

"Well, nice to meet you, Pierce. Nice to put a name on my bruises," he said.

Pierce arched his head to glare at Rafe and, without missing a beat, said, "You went looking for it, dude. You were the asshole that stole my suitcase—or tried to, anyway".

Rafe held his hands up, accepting defeat at Pierce's words. "You could, however, have just given me a light push and taken your bag. You didn't have to punch, kick, *and* spit on me."

"Hey," he turned again. "I did not spit on you. I spat next to you. It didn't even get you," he snapped.

"It could have, though," Rafe responded.

"I'm pretty good with my aim." He attempted to go back to his book, but Rafe wasn't gonna let him. He was enjoying their conversation. He enjoyed seeing Pierce's temper swelling up with his chest, trying to defend himself.

"What happened to you, anyway? Why were you naked in the middle of Central Park, washing a pullover?"

Pierce told him, once more, that it was none of his business.

"Okay, so I'll just assume you're a nudist," Rafe said, climbing up to his bed.

"Am not," he heard him reply with a muffled sound, a mattress separating them now.

Rafe laughed at the reply. "Your current…" He let the pause stir up the air before continuing, "attire is not helping your case. So allow me to assume you're a nudist. Or an exhibitionist. Or a nude exhibitionist."

He smirked when he heard Pierce take a deep breath and reply very quietly and dryly, "Fuck you."

"I would, but you're not my type," Rafe replied. Pierce exhaled.

"Don't flatter yourself. You're not my type either," Pierce commented.

Rafe wished that reply gave a clear clue as to whether Pierce was gay or not, but he would have to drown in the mystery for now.

Rafe opened his mouth to retort about being Pierce's type, but Pierce interrupted him before any sounds left his mouth.

"I wanna sleep, dude. Shut up!"

He felt the bed moving and heard the book slam shut.

"I thought you were waiting for your clothes to dry, nudist," Rafe said, covering himself with the blanket.

Pierce cursed, got up, put his shoes on, and headed for the door. He stopped, turned back, and pulled his suitcase from under the bed, taking it with him and slamming the door as he left.

"*Qué bruto*!" Rafe whispered and closed his eyes, his tiredness giving in to the soft cushion and taking him to dreamworld.

Chapter 5
Pierce

hen Pierce woke up, Rafe was still fast asleep. He hadn't talked to him since last night, when Rafe had reminded him to go get his clothes Pierce was still a little embarassed that he'd accidentally slammed the door on his way out. Rafe was a funny guy, albeit being a thief, but Picrce was in no mood to have a repeat of the conversation they'd had the previous night.

He collected all his items, as few as they were, and tiptoed out of the room. He visited the kitchen to help himself to some breakfast, not that much was provided. Just the bare essentials:

cereals and milk, pancake mix, coffee and tea, bread. He had a heap of cereal to start with while enjoying an instant coffee, then chucked a couple slices of bread into his suitcase before venturing into the city.

Coming out of the hostel, he headed toward the clothing store that he'd seen the night before. They had a few racks of coats on display outside. But Pierce was determined not to steal. He had the money.

He entered the store, and a young salesman approached him, inquiring about his needs. Pierce asked to be shown winter coats and their prices. The guy led him to the back of the facility where a wide selection of coats were laid out. He started pointing at each of them, quoting their best features and their price.

"This one has a fur lining so it's really warm," he said, showing him the brown inside of a black parka.

"Do you have anything not made of dead animals?" Pierce asked, disgusted at the idea of putting a carcass on his body, for the sake of getting warm, when he had other options. The only animal skin he allowed anywhere near him was his grandad's suitcase, and only because it was the only thing of his he owned.

The guy nodded and moved him a few feet to the left to show him more jackets. "This one has detachable sleeves, so it can be turned into a spring vest later on. Very functional. It's seventy-five dollars," he said holding up a black parka and then pointed at another. "This one is a bit lighter but warm nonetheless, and it's sixty dollars," the guy said.

Pierce was looking at his options and was starting to doubt his decision to enter the store. "Do you have anything on the cheaper side?"

"What's your budget?" the man asked, putting his hands together in front of his chest.

Pierce winced, calculating. "About twenty bucks," he said

The salesman grimaced. "I'm sorry, for that price I only have scarves and pashminas," he told him, putting his hands to his waist, clearly done doing business with Pierce. Pierce got the message.

"Thanks," he said exiting the store.

He walked to the other corner of the block and entered the donut store. A couple of Indian women with bindis painted between their brows greeted him. He approached the counter, refraining from looking at the goods they were selling. If he did, he'd buy a few, unable to resist his already growling stomach.

"Hi, I was wondering if you had any jobs," he asked.

One of the women, probably the manager,

left the counter and came to his side, eyeing him up and down. Her eyes settled on his worn sneakers and the faded jeans. She squinted. "You have a resumé?"

Pierce shook his head.

"Yeah, thought so. Well, print one out and bring it to me and if we have any openings I'll give you a call," she replied.

A call! A call! How was he supposed to receive phone calls when he didn't have a cell phone? What number would he put in his resumé, and how would he be contacted? He needed a phone. And a number. Fuck his life. He had already spent all his money on that hostel. He now wished he hadn't after all.

He thanked the lady opposite him and left the donut place, finding himself back on the streets. He began thinking of his options while trying to locate an internet café to write his resumé. How could he make himself reachable to employers?

He found a place nearby and sat down to use a computer for an hour. He'd never created a resumé before, so that was his first action. He Googled it and followed the instructions step by step.

Name: Pierce Callahan.

Birthdate: 02/15/1995.

E-mail address:

That was it. He had, completely by chance, found the way. He'd just give his e-mail. He hadn't used it in a while, so it would need a good clean-up to leave space for new and important e-mails, but he had one, and it was free, and accessing it was only a buck at the local internet café away.

He wrote down the address, then filled out the rest of the document with his details, education, and experience, which had been minimal. But every little bit was important. When he was done, he gave it a once over and printed a few copies. Then, he accessed his e-mail.

2,405 unread e-mails. Mostly junk. He deleted every single message, including the ones from the past, before he'd been kicked to the curb. Clean slate. That was what he needed.

He paid for his services and exited the café, reinvigorated with excitement, waving his resumés in his hand as he walked down the street. He would head downtown. It was where it was busiest in Manhattan and where there were surely more vacancies.

He saw a job ad taped on the window pane of a bar and he decided to pay it a visit. Only when he'd stepped inside had he realized he had never done this before and had no clue what to say or how to handle the situation. He decided to turn around and leave when someone from behind the bar greeted him.

"Hi," he answered reluctantly to the bartender.

"How can I help?" she asked with a wide smile.

He paused a second before replying. "I was just wondering if you have any jobs," he told her.

She nodded and went to get her manager to talk to him. Could it be that easy? Really? On his second try? He was trying not to overthink things before they actually took place; he didn't like getting disappointed.

A woman, older than the barmaid who had answered his question, came out of a door behind the bar and approached Pierce with vigor. The closer she came, though, the more her face changed, until eventually she stopped, the girl behind her bumping onto her. She looked at Pierce up and down, and without missing a beat she turned her head to the right, talking to her employee.

"Carol, why would you bring me to the front to interview a hobo? Seriously, I got more important things to do in the office," she said.

Pierce was as shocked as Carol. He'd washed his jumper, his trousers, had an extensive shower, cleaned up his hair, scrubbed his face, and given his grandpa's suitcase a once over.

How was it even possible he still looked what he was? Was it that obvious? Had he missed a spot that no one else did? What was it that screamed 'homeless' whenever a potential employer looked at him? He really wanted to know, if he was gonna change his living situation.

The manager turned to Pierce next and shouted with bitterness spilling out of her every pore. "Go sort your life out before you come asking me for a job."

That's what he was trying to do, for fuck's sake. Frustrated, he walked out of the bar. He kept south, heading toward the busier areas, although he already felt it was a lost battle. Two people had already given him the boot before he could even talk to them, and he doubted his chances looked any brighter in the Village.

So Pierce ventured into bars, clothing stores, restaurants, and everything else that looked remotely opportune, but no opportunity came his way. While most personnel he talked to were genuinely nice, their bosses didn't have the same stance. They were all weary of the 'hobo' the minute they set their eyes on him. Some looked at him with pity. Some with mere disgust. Most of them felt that it was their duty to advise him to fix his life. As if they had any clue what that entailed.

The more rejections he got, however, the

more determined he was. And hopeful. Hopeful that the next place he got in would at least interview him before giving him a pass. At the start of the day, he had printed fifteen copies of his resume. Thirty places later, he still had fifteen copies. It had been too long since he started, and he had missed lunch in favor of trying harder.

When he looked at the next store's clock, it was six p.m. He had spent an entire day being rejected. He was surprised he didn't want to kill himself. He wasn't going to quit just yet, however. Sure, he couldn't go on all day, but until the sun completely set, he would keep on trying.

His search had brought him all the way to Tribeca, and he decided to head back uptown and try his luck in all the places he'd missed. There were, what? A million stores in Manhattan? One must take him. If not in Manhattan, then Brooklyn or Queens or somewhere. He couldn't rot away before he had the chance to flourish. They couldn't do that to him. The world owed him that, at least, for having cursed him with societal hate and intolerance. It owed him a minuscule sliver of empathy. And he was determined to find that sliver.

In almost no time he was back in the northern part of the Village and walking around blocks he was certain he hadn't passed before.

He noticed a bistro with long, black, tall tables and white stools outside, mason jars filled with rose petals placed at equal intervals across its surface. On closer inspection, he noticed that the rose petals were glued on the glass surface and tealight candles lit up inside the jar. An oval-shaped sign on the wall right next to the glass entrance told him he was about to enter the establishment called Les Fourches.

The entire place was decorated in a similar minimalistic manner to the outside. Black and white furniture with mason jar candle holders and salt and pepper shakers placed next to each other made the whole place look cold and distant—except for the candlelight mixed with the yellow hue of the hanging light bulbs and the paintings lining every wall, which made him feel welcome.

It was a small place. He counted approximately fifteen tables. The bar on the left side was a dazzling view. Black and white granite made up the actual bar surface. The shelves on the wall housed all sorts of liquor in massive mason jars with little taps to pour the drink. The beer taps were barely visible behind the bar. The whole area was wired with fairy lights, making it look like a place that had sprung out of a drunk man's daydream. It was sheer perfection. He hardly stood a chance.

Three waiters were maneuvering around the tall tables, providing the patrons anything they required. A man, a decade or two older than Pierce, stood by the door behind the host stand, talking on the phone while scribbling something on a paper in front of him. He glanced at Pierce and signaled a moment with his finger while he finished up the call. Pierce took the opportunity to make more observations about the facility.

The waiters, all male, were tall and muscular, handsome and lean, but also quick on their feet and intelligent-looking. The bartender was a bit on the shorter side but buffer than anyone else, his muscles flexing as he shook the cocktail shaker. Everyone was clean-shaven and trimmed, their clothes ironed and tight around their body. They all wore gray, knee-length aprons and carried a smartphone in their hands when they weren't dealing with trays or food plates.

Everyone was smiling and gentle with their motions. The patrons, a majority of men and a few upperclass families, were all thin and well-dressed, as polished—perhaps even more if that was even possible—as the personnel. They all were busy talking to each other or gawking at their expensive gadgets while sipping or nibbling on something. He had walked into a lot of places, but Pierce felt this might be the one that made him feel the most awkward. The most out of place.

Sure he had the muscles to match the waiters', even if they were starting to lose their taut nature as was natural after months on the streets, but other than that he had nothing in common with these people. Not anymore, anyway. Coming from a deeply religious family, he probably was never exactly like them, anyway. But close enough.

He turned around to leave.

"Hi, table for one?" the host asked him before he could escape.

Pierce turned to the host with reluctance. He grimaced and paused. Only for a moment, however, before he placed his smile on his face and approached the stand.

"No, actually, I was looking for a job," he said, and his sweaty palm tightened around the handle of his suitcase.

"Okay. I might have an opening for a person. Do you have any experience?" he asked.

Pierce was dumbfounded. The guy hadn't given him a once over like all the others had. He was actually asking him a genuine question.

"Just a little. Bits and pieces over summer vacation and during college," he replied.

The guy nodded. "Okay. Okay. How old are you, kid?"

Pierce hesitated. He wasn't even sure if he could work in an alcohol-serving bar before he turned twenty-one. If he couldn't, he was doomed already. "Twenty," he said.

"All right. Do you have a resumé?" he asked.

Pierce was almost overcome with tears. He wanted a resumé. Was this place that had made him feel so out of place a few moments ago going to be his lucky charm? Pierce nodded and knelt down to retrieve one from inside his suitcase. He felt the eyes of the guy heating the back of his head. He got one out, closed his suitcase, and stood up.

The guy's eyes were slitted now. He was calculating something. He didn't take Pierce's resumé when he held it out to him. Just stared at Pierce.

"Are you homeless, kid?"

There it was. The question that he dreaded being asked despite not having been asked it before. Everyone either assumed it or deduced he was. No one had asked him yet. It was his time to lie. But when he opened his mouth, he found he couldn't do it.

"Yes," he said and lowered his head.

The guy shook his head and grimaced. "I'm sorry, kid. I can't hire someone like you, in your state. Come back when you've sorted yourself out," he said in a very fatherly tone that brought memories to Pierce. Memories he wasn't very pleased with. Memories of his own father telling him what an abomination he was. Memories of his father pushing him out of the door, while he struggled to grab everything and anything that he could.

The anger blinded him that instant, and he didn't hold back. "Come back when I've sorted myself out?" he scoffed. "You know how many times I've heard this today? Do you? Of course you don't. You all think you're so much better than me. You all think you know everything about me. You take one look, and you see the hobo you don't trust. You see a junkie. A pathetic crazy person. You see a beggar. A criminal. A delinquent. Right? Am I right?"

The guy barely nodded, still in shock of being confronted by the homeless kid he had rejected.

"But you see, looks deceive, don't they? You were going to give me a chance before you saw the suitcase, my shoes, my clothes, whatever the fuck it is that gives me away, even though I've made myself presentable."

He noticed a few of the patrons had turned to look.

"But no. You have to tell me to go and sort myself out. Like I don't know that. Like that is not what I'm trying to do. Like that isn't the reason I'm out, spending whatever money I've managed to make to print my resumé so I can go and ask for a fucking job. I could have bought a coat, a blanket, something valuable so I don't die out in the cold *fucking* winter that is coming. But no. I chose to do this. And you have the nerve to tell me to go and sort myself out. Tell me, how is a homeless kid, rejected by his family because of his sexuality, with no security, no one to take care of him, supposed to sort himself out, if no one will fucking hire him?"

His anger had dissipated as he vented. When he finished, he felt breathless and cold. His stomach pulsed and his head felt light as he came to the realization that everyone was now staring at him and he had embarrassed himself. Tears started shaping in his eyes. Before he made an even bigger fool of himself, he decided to leave.

He heard the guy say as he opened the door, "If you can come to work washed, clean-shaven, and with ironed clothes, you can start next Friday."

Pierce froze in his position, the tears finally releasing onto his cheeks. He wiped them before he turned to look at the bar manager. "You...you mean that?"

"I only have a need for a weekender, so

I can only give you two, maybe three shifts a week, but only if you can come to work like I said," the guy told him. "And I'm not being an asshole, but I really can't..."

"Thank you," Pierce cut him off. "That's enough for me. Thank you," he repeated and his eyes stung as they were threatened by the invasion of more tears.

"What's your name, kid?" he asked.

"Pierce. Callahan," he said, thrusting his resumé out. The manager took it.

"Well, Pierce, I'm Vance," he said and reached into his pocket. He took something out and passed it to Pierce. "Here. Go buy yourself some clothes from somewhere. I'm sorry for being such a dick before," he said.

Pierce felt the bills in his hand but couldn't believe how good the man he'd just screamed at had turned out to be. "You made up for it by being such an angel. Thank you. I'll see you next Friday," he said and opened the door to leave for the third time.

"Oh, what time do you want me here?" he asked.

***

"I know it's a lot to ask, but can you please do that for me? It will be the first and last time,"

Pierce was sitting at the reception desk opposite the hostel staff member.

He had come with a plan on his way back and now was trying to implement it. Someone had given him a chance and he didn't want to let him down. Someone had believed in him when his own blood couldn't.

"I'm sorry. It's our policy. We don't accept last minute cancelations," the guy said. He was Asian. Chinese from what Pierce could tell, with near-perfect English. He was rather chubby in the face, but quite adorable nonetheless. He'd be a stud if he let him have his way, though.

"Come on, man. Level with me. I've been out all day looking for a job. No one even gave me a second look, and then finally, this guy — this *angel* — gave me an opportunity. All I ask is that I transfer the second night I paid for to next Thursday so I can come here to clean up and turn up for my first job with the same respect he's given me," he told him.

The receptionist grimaced, twitched his mouth, then rolled his eyes. "Okay. But don't tell anyone I did that. It could cost *me* my own job."

Pierce smiled broadly. It seemed Vance had the magic touch. He felt like he could accomplish anything at that moment. He sprang up, planted a kiss in the guy's cheek, and strolled out of the hostel with his suitcase and his dignity intact. Life was good!

Of course, it had to be that moment he came to the realization that the temperature outside had dropped considerably. Describing it as lightly chilly would be the understatement of the year. It was motherfucking cold. It was the clear return to reality, his reality. He might have found a job, but it would be more than a couple of months before he could rent a room. He didn't even know what he would be paid, if the place had good tips. It looked like it should. It was a classy bistro in the Village. It'd be crazy if it didn't. But he would still have to live on the streets most nights to save money for an actual room.

He felt like punching himself. What the fuck was wrong with him? Why was he focusing on all the cons? What had happened to him? He used to be such a positive person. A healthy man with a passion for his body and an empathy for the planet he lived on. He was a recycler, an energy and water saver, and a vegan bodybuilder in the making. To an outsider's eye, he would be the epitome of a hipster, coming from a middle-class Christian family from Upstate New York. But he was nothing like his parents. They were the reason he'd become so pessimistic. Before they kicked him out, he was his own man. Now, he was a nobody at the mercy of the kindness of strangers.

No. Pierce dismissed the negativity for now. He was going look at everything good about his life at that particular moment. He had a job. In a few months, he'd have a room, hopefully sooner if it paid well. His *own* room. Maybe next year he could resume college too. If to have all that he had to sleep wherever he could for another month or so, he would brave the winter. He would sleep in the subway. He would sleep at Central Park. He wouldn't even care if he'd get pissed on or mugged again. If that's what it took to kick start his life, he would do it.

A shout permeated his ears and he turned to find the source. He couldn't see anything, but a second scream guided him down the road he was walking and in to an alley between two apartment buildings. Two men were knelt on the ground pinning someone from the hands and legs while a third guy was unbuttoning the victim's trousers, shutting his mouth with his hand.

The victim was also a guy. Pierce knew because he tried to ungag his mouth and grunted.

"Shut the fuck up, boy. When you give up your ass, you ain't screaming."

"Hey!" Pierce shouted at the guys before he could control himself.

The guy who was doing the unbuttoning turned and, seeing Pierce, stood up. Pierce etched closer. The only streetlight in the alley hit the victim's face and Pierce recognized it. It was Rafe.

Chapter 6
Rafe

hat do you want?" the *cabrón* asked. The one who had started all this.

"I think it's pretty clear the guy doesn't want your dick in his mouth," his potential savior said, "Frankly, I understand his sentiment. So, why don't you let him go?"

Rafe couldn't see his face. The streetlight behind him only gave him a silhouette but no features.

"Run along, boy. You *don't* wanna get involved in this," the *cabrón* said. He was a five-foot-something man with a cap on and a young face. He had big muscles and a generally big physique. The guy across from him didn't stand a chance. He was tall and much thinner.

"Oh, something tells me I *really* wanna get involved in this. I also have the feeling this is gonna end badly for some of you." The guy paused, then continued with a chuckle. "Don't—don't you get the same feeling? Is it just me?"

Rafe's brusque attacker wasn't having any of the attitude. "*Papi*," he said, hitting his fist on his palm, "you better run away now or you'll regret this."

"Ooh, I'm scared," the guy said derisively. "But, honestly, that feeling is telling me that *you* will be the one to regret this. Isn't that weird? I don't know about you, but I want to put the feeling to the test," he said and let down his briefcase.

Rafe looked closer. As the guy bent down, the light touched him briefly and he saw blue piercing eyes. And then the light hit the briefcase, which turned out to be a small suitcase. Could it—could it really be Pierce? Was he so fortunate? When the *gillipollas* started running toward him, though, Rafe wished it wasn't Pierce. He didn't want him involved in his life. He didn't want him hurt in his defense. He didn't want that beautiful face ruined by the stitches he'd have to get after that asshole was done with him.

The *cholo* charged at Pierce with a fist raised in the air. Pierce took a few steps forward, hunched, and forced his arm in the guy's stomach, avoiding his punch in the process. He swept the other guy's legs out from under him, bringing him to the ground with a thud. The *cholo* groaned. Pierce punched him in the face several times until he lost the strength to fight back.

"*Hijo de puta*," said the guy pinning Rafe's legs, and he felt the release of the pressure in his ankles as he stood to confront Pierce.

He raised his palms in front of him, protecting his face, and called to Pierce, provoking him. Pierce didn't take long to catch the bait. He left the short guy to lick his wounds and walked towards the other attacker, who stood almost as tall as Pierce himself. But Pierce didn't attack him. He waited, jumping left and right, waiting.

Seconds later, Rafe heard the second guy roar as he aimed a punch toward Pierce. Pierce ducked and pushed the arm away from him. Then kicked the guy's groin, which had been left wide open and unprotected.

Rafe decided to help the situation. He was sure once Pierce knocked the second guy down, the third one would go looking for the same kind of fate his friends were suffering. But not if he could help. Since his legs were free now and the third guy was holding his hands above him with such strength, it only took a clumsy somersault for Rafe to place his foot straight into the guy's face and land on his feet like Catwoman. He pushed his knee up into the guy's stomach to knock him senseless, and when that didn't do much, he imitated his savior and melted the man's balls with his foot.

"I told ya I had a feeling, guys," Pierce commented as he dusted his hands.

Rafe looked on the ground where the second man was lying, lamenting his new-found impotence. Chuckling loudly, Pierce approached Rafe. He was suddenly overwhelmed with the cold, and his knees trembled. His legs gave out on him when Pierce took him in his arms.

"Are you okay, Rafe?" he asked. Rafe nodded. "Can you walk?" Rafe nodded again. "Okay, let's go, buddy. Before they try anything foolish again."

Pierce put Rafe's arm around his neck and his own arm around Rafe's back and grabbed his suitcase with his free hand.

He carried Rafe back to the main street and then led him to the closest avenue. Rafe felt Pierce's fingertips massaging the back of his hand. He didn't say anything, however. He kept quiet and kept looking back to make sure the assholes weren't following.

They were on Frederick Douglass Avenue in no time. When they were hit by the bright city lights, he asked Rafe if he was okay to walk on his own. Rafe replied positively and lifted whatever weight he had leaned on Pierce to support himself. They headed south, walking at a slow pace, passing by closing stores and dimly lit side streets.

"How are you feeling? Did those bastards manage to hurt you before I got there?" Pierce whispered next to him.

"No," Rafe shook his head. "Not really. You were there just in time. My savior." Rafe smiled at Pierce. Pierce avoided his gaze.

"What happened back there?" he said instead.

Rafe calculated his words before he spoke them. He was too embarrassed to admit to Pierce that he was a rentboy, a prostitute. He already thought lowly of him. He didn't want to sink the bar even lower.

"Nothing. They saw me walking down the street and started catcalling me and following me. Then they pushed me into the alley. The rest, you know," he said.

"I hate people. On most days," Pierce commented and he halted his pacing in front of a 24/7 cafe just a block away from Central Park.

"Come," he said, "I'll buy you coffee."

Rafe didn't hesitate to follow him inside the orange-tinted place and take a seat by the window display. Not only had he saved him from rape, he was buying him coffee too. The more times he encountered Pierce, the more gentlemanly he seemed to be.

"So…how are things?" Rafe asked, putting an end to the uncomfortable silence that had been lingering between them since they'd taken a seat.

Pierce nodded. "Things are great. I just managed to get a part-time job," he said.

Rafe smiled. "That's incredible. How did that happen? Where?" he asked, as the waitress stopped in front of them, leaving two glasses of water on their table and taking their order. Rafe ordered his hot cocoa and Pierce a cup of drip coffee.

As soon as the waitress left to prepare their drinks, he replied, "I went around town asking for a job, and this amazing guy gave me one after like, a ton of rejections. It's in a bistro bar down at the Village."

"That's cool. Lucky you," Rafe answered.

Pierce thanked him, and his cheeks flushed as he smiled. His eyes avoided Rafe's gaze, looking instead at the still water in front of him. How cute. Rafe was convinced that Pierce was once as sweet as he appeared now, and that the situations that brought him to the streets had made him the guy he'd seen the first time he met him. Stealing aside.

"So you're gonna be leaving the streets now, right?" Rafe asked.

Pierce sipped his water and finally turned his eyes to the man across him. "I hope so. As soon as I get enough money to rent a room," he replied.

"That's incredible, Pierce. When you do, don't forget us lost souls."

Pierce shook his head. "I would never. I've spent enough time on the streets to carry the experience for life," he replied with a depth to his voice. A depth that radiated with Rafe. He knew what he was talking about. It was a weight they would both carry for life, even if Rafe managed to get off the streets, which he deemed unlikely. He would probably die before he could have a family, a life again. The thought brought his *madre* to his mind and how heartbreaking it'd be for her if she never saw her son again. He had a job as well. He just needed to get better at it, if he was to leave the streets and reunite with his mother in the future.

He realized he hadn't spoken for a while and tried to refocus on the man in front of him. Pierce was gazing at the road outside, seemingly undisturbed by the quiet between them. He appeared relaxed, calm even, considering he had just handed a group of thugs their asses. He was charming. A man's man.

To Rafe, Pierce didn't look particularly macho with his sunken cheeks and his immature stubble. However, he gave off an air of security. It was probably the fact that he had just saved him, but if Rafe had a say in it, he wouldn't leave this guy's side for the world.

Their drinks arrived, and the smell of cocoa hit Rafe's nostrils, bringing his sense of safety full circle. He felt at home. All that was missing was Marissa and his *madre,* and he would be the happiest man in the world.

Pierce concentrated on his coffee and the traffic outside more than he did on Rafe. Not that he was ignoring him. He acknowledged his presence, but Rafe assumed he was a man of few words. Rafe wasn't, and he would be damned if he didn't find out more about this guy now that he had the chance.

"What's in the suitcase? You carry it everywhere you go. Isn't it uncomfortable to take it around town? Why don't you get a rucksack. That way you can at least put it around your back?"

Rafe realized a little too late that maybe he had overdone it with the questions. Pierce didn't seem bothered by it, though. He turned his attention to Rafe and answered.

"It's a family heirloom. It belonged to my grandad. He passed it to me when he died, so it's got sentimental value."

"I see…I think," Rafe answered, trying to sound more sure of himself, but he still couldn't see the point. He had nothing; he was carrying around that damned suitcase even though it was impractical.

Pierce breathed out as if contemplating whether to continue, took a sip of his coffee, and explained. "My gramps was gay too. But he was late to reveal the truth to his family. It took him sixty-five years. And when he did, my family wrote him off. He was a castaway, no longer welcome in his house. He went on to travel, away from his wife, his kids. He lived a good life as a gay man. He traveled every inch of this world and back. I only saw him once after his coming out, and that was on his funeral. Later on, his attorney read his will to us all. He'd left nothing to anyone, but me. And all he had to give me was his suitcase.

"My parents told me I couldn't have it and kept it locked away for years. But when I turned eighteen, I turned the whole house upside down and found it. There was a lock on it, and his attorney had given the key only to me at his funeral. So thankfully my parents hadn't been able to throw away anything sinful in the suitcase and ruin my grandad's memories. But that was all I had left of him, and it was enough because whatever was inside made me feel normal, like I wasn't a freak. Like I could be loved if I was truthful to myself. It's what eventually drove me to come out to my parents. I thought they would have learned from their past mistakes, but they hadn't. And here I am," he said.

Rafe smiled. Now he got it. That suitcase was a reminder of all he was and all he could be, just like his *madre* was for him. Sure, one was an actual person, but they both had the same effect. Made them feel like they weren't all that alone or all that fucked up.

Pierce called the waitress with a wave of his hand, pushing his chair back. "Wanna go?"

"Sure," Rafe answered reluctantly. Where would he go now? It was already very late, and there was probably no traffic on his street. He'd have to spend yet more money from his fund to stay at a hostel. He didn't see another option.

"Got anywhere to stay tonight?" Pierce asked stepping out of the cafeteria.

Rafe pointed at nowhere in particular. "I was gonna go stay at a hostel," he said.

"I'll walk you," Pierce said casually heading down the road. Rafe caught up with his quick pace.

"You really don't have to," he told him.

Pierce shook his head. "It's not a problem. So where to? Got anywhere in particular? I know a cheap place around the corner," Pierce said, again avoiding Rafe's eyes.

"Lead the way," Rafe laughed, leaving them in quiet.

Rafe found it hilarious, how Pierce could go so long without talking. "Do you always talk this much, Pierce, or are you just shy around me?" he laughed.

Pierce stole some glances towards Rafe. He smiled. "Sorry. Bad habit. I'm not used to talking to anyone."

Rafe winced. "You don't have any friends on the streets?" Could he really be all that alone out in NYC?

Pierce shook his head. "Nah, can't trust anyone."

"Ouch!" Rafe commented and Pierce turned at him to apologize.

"I mean, it's hard trusting someone when everyone's looking out for themselves," Pierce tried to justify himself.

Rafe stopped him in his tracks and looked in his eyes. "That's a lonely way of thinking."

Pierce looked to the pavement and didn't say a thing.

"Sorry," Rafe said. "I just feel bad that you don't have anyone to talk to about your worries and dreams," he told Pierce and continued their walk.

"What's the point? Worries: where will I sleep? What will I eat? Dreams: When will I win the lottery and get the hell outta here?"

"There's much more to friends than that, Pierce," Rafe said.

They stopped in front of the hostel that Pierce had stayed the previous night. Pierce opened the door for Rafe and they both walked to the reception. Rafe asked for a bed and the receptionist told him they had one available for thirty-five bucks. Rafe bit his lip. That was half what he made a night. It was too much, but he couldn't just walk out. Not when Pierce had insisted on walking him and making sure he was safe.

"Sure," Rafe said and unhooked his rucksack from his back and loosened the string. Before he had any time to pull out his stash, Pierce pulled some bills out of his pocket and gave them to the receptionist. He paused before letting them go. "No, Pierce. You don't have to do that. Really," Rafe begged him, stopping the receptionist from putting the money away.

"It's okay, Rafe," Pierce said and walked out of the hostel. Rafe took the money out of the receptionist's hand and followed Pierce, excusing himself.

"Wait up. Pierce!" he was standing outside when Rafe came out the door waiting for Rafe. "You don't have to give your money to me. I can…" he started to say, pressing the bills, and his hand, to Pierce's chest, but Pierce cut him off.

"Rafe, stop. I want to do this. I-I want you to be safe. Especially after such a stupid night," Pierce said, staring at the traffic and pushing Rafe's hand off his chest. The man was playing so tough — and he was, kicking everyone's butt to prove as much — but ask him to talk about his feelings, and he blushed.

"Well," Rafe said, stepping in front of Pierce to force him to look him in the eyes and finish what he wanted to say. "Thank you. You… There's a sweetheart under that brute after all," he told him and placed a kiss on his cheek. "Don't be a stranger, stranger."

Rafe disappeared back inside the hostel and got his keys from the receptionist.

"He your boyfriend?" the receptionist asked, giving him a purple key ring with a number written on it.

Rafe smiled. "I wish." He grabbed the keys and went to bed.

Chapter 7
Rafe

Sleep had been impossible that night, although the warmth had been welcome. It wasn't often that a hostel was heated. But that did nothing for Rafe's busy mind while attempting to rest. Every time he closed his eyes, he would see the *cholos* that had attacked him in the alley. And he would see Pierce coming to his rescue and kicking ass, but whenever he thought peacefulness would be next, there would be the face of his abusers. Again. And again. Until the sun came up and he had to check out. Not before exploiting the breakfast provided with a stay, however.

He walked aimlessly with nothing planned

for the day. He had nothing planned for most days. Only at nights. He wished he had his canvases and his oils. Hell, even a sketchbook would be nice right now, instead of going nowhere.

The more he craved a pencil and a piece of paper, the more it brought adolescent memories in his head. It didn't seem to want to stop. Everything hurtful he had ever experienced, no matter how small, was coming to the forefront now.

He remembered when he came home with homework for art class from school and he got to paint all day. It had been the first time he had devoted his time to creating something from scratch, and he found it so calm, so soothing, that it had been midnight before he even realized it. He had been fourteen at the time. He never had a curfew or anything, but his parents would always nag when he was still out of bed at a late time. That day his dad came in his bedroom and started shouting about him wasting his time all day instead of doing his homework. When he defended himself, his dad gave him a good whooping and told him to straighten up and go to bed.

It was that time he realized he might like drawing more than he initially thought. He started drawing everywhere he went, everywhere he sat. He bought sketchbooks with his pocket money.

In a matter of a month it was full. His dad always complained when he saw him drawing. But he enjoyed it, both drawing and being nagged at. His dad despising his hobby meant his dad spent less time complaining about the other quirks of his son. Like that he was skinny and not playing any sports at school. Like the fact that he loved pink, or that he'd put up posters of his favorite divas on his walls. Everything was obscured by all the sissy drawing. It was comforting, no matter how weird it might sound.

When he looked up from his thoughts, he found he was halfway across Manhattan, at a place he had never been before, and with an arts store calling him from across the street. He laughed. Life was such a weirdo sometimes. The way it worked you up. The way it mocked you.

He crossed the street and went inside. He bought a small sketchbook and a couple pens and pencils. To heck with his savings. He'd missed drawing. Having nothing to do for the rest of the day, he found his way to Mario's and sat inside, filling in the pages of his new possession. He was so involved in his activity that he let his hot cocoa run cold, a sin of biblical proportions in his book.

He felt a cold hand on his shoulder and he jumped. It was Sonia.

"Sorry, sweetie, didn't mean to scare

you. Are you okay? You haven't said a word in the—" she looked at the clock on the wall and calculated—"three hours you've been here. You haven't even touched your cocoa. Is it not good? Do you want another one?" Her eyes were wide with concern and her lips sucked in, forming a thin pale line.

He nodded. "I'm good, Sonia. Thanks. I'm just…I don't know…I guess it has been so long since I've had a pen and paper that I got carried away," he replied, and she smiled. Rafe could tell just by the change in her eyes' size. "I'll take your offer on the cocoa, though," he said.

"Okay, but you better drink this one, or I'll call the meds to get you tested," she chortled as she walked back to the counter.

"Gotcha," Rafe replied and resumed his drawing. It had been three hours, yet it felt like only minutes since he'd sat down. He looked at what he'd been drawing. He hadn't decided on anything before he started, but his hands had shaped a human body and then added the details, and looking at it now, the almost-finished piece looked so much like Pierce he was astounded by both his lingering talent and his photographic memory concerning the man.

What had Pierce done to him? He seemed to be the one anchor that his mind went back to every time it remembered a traumatic experience.

This kickass, macho, shy man who didn't speak much but blushed a lot was making his stomach ache, but in a good way. As if it would hold his breath captive until they saw each other again.

"Oh, who's that? Your boyfriend?" Sonia sang as she put another cup next to Rafe. Rafe saw her looking at his pad.

"No. I wish," he answered. What was wrong with him? Why did he keep saying that about Pierce every time someone asked him? He knew he wouldn't stand a chance with Pierce. They were both homeless and hopeless. Even if they did manage to get something going, how long would it last before Rafe kicked it? He was sick, and without money he would eventually die.

He downed his cocoa and decided to color Pierce in.

A hand pulled his notebook down, making him jump again. This time it was Marissa.

"Hey, guuurl!" she said, taking a seat across him. "Whatcha doing?" She peeked at Rafe's half-colored Pierce and hummed. "Mm, who is this hottie?"

"No one," Rafe said before he could express it as a wish like he'd done twice before.

"What's up with you?" Marissa asked.

Sonia approached the table again and put down a cup of tea in front of her. "Oh, he's been like that all day. I think someone is in love," she said, prancing back to her counter.

Marissa laughed. "Is that true?"

He shook his head. Just because he'd drawn a guy he'd met and really liked didn't mean he was in love. Just because he was sitting in silence not touching his hot drink didn't mean he was infatuated.

"C'mon. You can tell me if you are. Who is it?" Marissa insisted, asking what he was like and where he met him. Rafe was getting sick of the interrogation. He felt his blood rising inside of him and his skin getting hot.

"I'm not in love, Marissa. I was nearly raped, for fuck's sake," he scoffed at her, making sure to not shout loud enough to be heard all across the store.

Marissa pushed herself back in her chair. "What? How? What happened?"

"Some assholes saw me trying to pick up customers and started following me. They pushed me in an alley and pinned me to the ground," Rafe murmured.

"Did they…?" Marissa couldn't and wouldn't finish her sentence, but Rafe was okay with that. Even he didn't like the sound of it spoken out loud, no matter if the word circled round and round his mind.

"No, they didn't. I said nearly. This guy

came in the alley and stopped them," he told her and sipped his chocolate.

Marissa reached for his hand across the table. "How do you feel? Can I…?" she started, but Rafe had enough talking about last night's incident.

He withdrew his hand from under hers. "I'm…okay, I guess. I will be okay. There's nothing you can do for me anyway," he said. Only when he said it did he realize it might have come across in a different way.

If Marissa was hurt, she didn't let it show because her hand stayed where it was on the table and her voice was as sympathetic as it had been before.

"Let me know if there's anything I can do, no matter how small," she told him.

Why wouldn't she drop the subject already? Rafe set his drink down, spilling some on his hand as he retaliated on Marissa. "Can you find me a home? No. How about a job that doesn't include me selling my body to creepy old dudes? No. Can you give me my medication or a medical insurance? No. So how the fuck do you think you can help me, Marissa?"

Was Pierce rubbing off on him or what? Where had that come from? He loved Marissa like a sister and didn't want to hurt her feelings, but there he was, throwing insults at her face, totally unprovoked. "I'm sorry," he managed to say before he dashed out of Mario's with his head hanging low in shame.

He wandered the streets thinking of how terrible he'd been to his best friend. Thinking of last night's events and how they brought the need for safety back into his life. He couldn't keep doing what he did because it was risky, but if he didn't, he'd die. How had his life got so fucked up?

The more he walked, the more upset he got with himself. His stomach tied up in knots as he kept telling himself what an idiot he'd been and how stupidly he had acted. He didn't know what had gotten into him. He wasn't like that. He was always nice to people. He was always nice to his parents, even though they were far less than that to him. He'd just take the hit. Literally.

His stomach bloated and his mouth felt dry and his knees wavered. He kept walking, but he felt weaker. His throat became hoarse and tingly. He coughed. He coughed again. Once he started, he was unable to stop.

He sat on a ledge, steadying himself, trying to soothe whatever had awakened inside. He took a deep breath, then another one. Sweat trickled down from his hairline to his forehead and down his eyebrow. His cheeks felt flushed. His body had calmed down, though, despite feeling warmer and warmer.

He took another breath, and the city pollution traveled up his nose and down his lungs, causing him to cough again. He covered his mouth and eyed the passersby, hoping he hadn't alarmed anyone. Rafe looked at his hand and found it was covered in sprinkles of blood. He put his finger in his mouth and took it out to inspect it. There was no blood. Where the hell had it come from?

His breathing became harder and he felt more sweat encompassing him. A feeling of sickness found its way to his mouth and he spewed vomit beside him. He coughed a little more, then wiped his mouth. The oxygen his nostrils inhaled seemed fresher now, and a coolness reached out to his limbs. He found his footing again, slowly but steadily.

Chapter 8
Pierce

Pierce opened his eyes, craning his neck to both sides, trying to ease the pain in his neck. Sleeping with a pillow under his neck was no longer a habit, so whenever it happened, it hurt his whole back. Not that he wasn't welcoming the soft feeling under him and the warmth surrounding him.

He had a quick shower in the same dingy bathroom he had used before and went down to the common room for breakfast. He took his time this morning, not being in any particular rush. His plans were all set, and he knew exactly what was going to happen, so his nerves were at ease and his brain fully concentrated on the one difficult thing he had to do today: work.

He waved at the receptionist, a hipster with dreads who was too far into reading a book to acknowledge him with more than a nod. He was okay with it. They had spent all last night talking about the possibility of him coming back later tonight and grabbing a last minute bed, whether it'd be possible to hold the same dorm for him. He thought since it was a different guy, he could try his luck at pushing things again. The guy had told him he'd do his best and promised to try his hardest to keep the two-bed dorm empty for the night. That was good enough for Pierce.

He went out into the street. Although it was a late October day, he was greeted by warmth and blinding sunlight. He smiled as he headed up the street. He walked for almost thirty minutes before reaching his destination. A clothing store called Market Deals spread out across the block in red, and typical New York foot traffic rushed in and out of the store.

He might have spent all his boss's money on Rafe's hostel last week, but he didn't regret it one bit, and he had even managed to make an honorable twenty-nine bucks in begging, trying to compensate for the money he'd lost and not willing to turn up at work in the same clothes and prove to his boss that he was a hopeless junkie, after all. He now had a bit over forty dollars to spend on clothes, and the first thing he'd grab was a coat. It might be a sunny day today, but that wouldn't last for long.

He walked in and grabbed a cart, placing his suitcase inside it. He rolled around, following the signs to the men's section.

He needed a thick enough jacket to ward off the cold on the nights he'd be sleeping outside or in the subway, but one that could easily be tucked away into his suitcase and still leave enough space to put some extra tees in.

He was struck by how many options he had and how cheap everything was. He tried more than a dozen coats, assessing them for all their flaws and pros and narrowed it down to two. One was stylish, had a flannel coating inside that made it extra warm, and had enough pockets in and out to fit in a small armada of knick-knacks. It was navy blue with brown buttons and cords and reached his thighs. The other one was a black parka with cotton stuffing and a few pockets, but otherwise less practical for anything other than sleeping outside. It was easily washable, however, made from polyester. He eyed the clock on the wall and decided not to waste any more time on making a decision his brain had already made ages ago. He picked up the navy blue coat and marched to the T-shirt section. Yes, it was more difficult to wash, but it made him look less homeless and more hipster, which in his situation was a good thing.

The T-shirts he found were on a bargain. Three for twenty dollars, plus fifteen dollars for the coat gave him some extra change to spare. He picked up a red comic-book themed tee and two artsy ones, black with white creative strokes and floral lettering, which he deemed perhaps more appropriate for a workplace environment.

Making his way to the registers, he noticed the shoe section and a big flashing card that read '$5 ONLY', which, of course, attracted his attention. He looked down to his shoes. While the wear and tear in his jeans made them look trendy, the same didn't apply for his Allstars. The soles had long separated from the rest of the shoe, only hanging onto a bit of glue, his laces were all muddied up, and the fabric was full of holes where his socks were visible. He needed new ones, but he always put them last on his list, always deeming the coat more important.

He browsed the shoe shelves and found a pair of red and white sneakers. He found his size, the last in that design, and carried everything to the register. The woman rang everything up for him, and once he'd paid he went to the corner of the street, took off his old shoes, threw them in the garbage can, and put on the new ones. The change in the arch of his feet felt strange. The balls and toes of his feet had grown so used to the discomfort of holes and bumps that being massaged while in motion seemed out of the ordinary, inhumane even. Shoes surely didn't feel so comfortable.

He started his journey down Malcolm X Avenue. He checked the clock inside a convenience store and realized it was still early. He was supposed to start in three hours, so he slowed his pace, enjoying a good stroll after a long time, feeling refreshed. He didn't want to admit it, but shopping made him feel good about himself. Elevated. Shopping therapy was a thing of the past. He was happy he had indulged in it after almost half a year. It had been that long. He had changed a lot since. But he'd be lying to himself if he didn't admit that he hadn't thoroughly enjoyed the excursion for necessities. Matched with the elation of starting a job, this was the best day he had ever had out on the streets.

"Hey, *bruto*," he heard someone say very close to him, and an a lift of his head revealed none other than Rafe.

"Hey," he said, feeling his lips part as they formed a smile out of their own volition. "How are you? How has it been since…?" He left the last bit of his question to hang in the air, not particularly keen to remind Rafe of that night.

"Good, good. Much…quieter, let's say. How about you? Been shopping, I see," he said looking at the plastic bags and the new flashy shoes.

"I was just heading to work. I had to buy a few things so I don't turn up looking like a hobo on my first day," Pierce explained.

Rafe nodded. "That's cool. I like the shoes. It was good seeing you. Enjoy work," he added, backtracking, moving away from Pierce hesitantly.

Pierce grimaced for a second, his mind processing the prospect of spending more time with Rafe. Before he got too far he called out to him. "Wanna walk with me? Get something to eat? I'll buy. I think," he said, remembering he'd spent the spare money he was supposed to have for food on the shoes.

"Um, are you sure? I don't wanna keep you from work or anything," Rafe replied. His face brightened up in an instant at Pierce's suggestion.

Pierce nodded, noticing the change in Rafe. His stomach curled. He could see the street rub off Rafe's face and be replaced with the cuteness of looking forward to something. "Sure. I've still got time. I'm not sure if I have money, but time, I've got plenty," he chuckled, and Rafe approached him, walking together.

Pierce counted his change. "I've got enough for ice cream," he admitted, noticing an ice cream van parked in the street in front of the north side of Central.

"Ice cream sounds fun." Rafe's lips arched, exposing his white teeth, a beautiful smile that gave Pierce goosebumps.

He'd buy him all the ice cream if it'd make him smile like that all the time.

Chapter 9
Rafe

o, what's your flavor?" he asked with a smirk.

Rafe was taken aback by the question, for a moment contemplating replying to the double entendre in a publicly unacceptable way. Then he decided against it as they approached the ice cream truck, which housed an older, Indian man with gray hair waiting to get paid by a mom.

"I like vanilla and Oreo. Just pure perfection," he answered and hummed with pleasure at the image in his head.

Pierce laughed. "I love Oreo too. But my favorite hands down is chocolate. I love milk chocolate. It was so hard giving it up," he commented as they stood in the small line to be served.

"Why did you have to give it up?" Rafe asked, his brain already at work, trying to figure out why someone would give up something they love.

"I became vegan," came his reply in a casual manner.

"Oh. Okay. I guess," Rafe commented.

Pierce squinted at Rafe's attempt of sounding approving.

"I just don't get why you would cut something out of your life if you loved it so much," Rafe explained, trying to sound as nonjudgmental as possible.

Pierce looked him in the eyes with a semi-serious face and eyes full of surprise. "I don't know. Why don't you ask my parents?"

Rafe cursed as he realized what he'd just said and apologized.

"Relax," Pierce laughed. "I was joking, dude. Well, sorta."

They finally reached the ice cream man and Pierce ordered for the two of them. He ordered two of Rafe's favorites and gave the man all his bills, leaving without his change. Was he trying to impress Rafe? Or was he, a homeless guy, hopeless with money in his hands? Rafe didn't care. He enjoyed this *bruto*'s company, and he would savor it and whatever benefits it came with for as long as he could.

He licked the cold dessert, and his taste buds were permeated by a blast of sweet wetness. He'd missed the taste of ice cream. He tried to avoid cold stuff to build up his immune system, not that it did anything. His immune system was fucked up. Completely. But if he could avoid catching pneumonia, he would. He didn't have a death wish.

"But seriously, it wasn't as hard as I thought it'd be. It was easy at first, then as the diet kicks in you start craving some of the crap you used to eat, but you fight through the cravings or supplement them with the closest equivalent, and then you're set. Honestly, this doesn't taste as good as it does in my memory," Pierce went on.

"So, you're still vegan? Or…" Rafe asked looking poignantly at the ice cream in Pierce's hands.

Pierce coughed. "God, no. I tried the first couple of weeks after I was kicked out, and I almost starved to death. That was before I came down to NYC. I'd get a couple of good souls willing to buy me food, but whenever I asked for something non-meaty, non-cheesy, they'd think I was being an ungrateful bastard. When you got no money and you are hungry, not knowing when your next meal is going to be, you get what you can to get by. Plus, most things I want to eat are more expensive. So when it's going to be famine or a dollar hot dog, I chose the dog.

"But I've met some vegetarians who are homeless and will not eat anything else. It doesn't work for me. If it does for them, I have no clue. Although, to be honest, now that I'm used to the city and how it works, whenever I have the option and money I do eat at least vegetarian…"

Rafe could hear him talking for hours, on whatever topic it was he wanted to go on about. He seemed to be passionate about his dietary needs.

If he was being honest to himself, he wasn't paying as much attention to the content of Pierce's words but to his tone and his emotions that were so generously pouring out as he explained his experience. Pierce seemed to be the guy with the constant resting bitch face, which only came off whenever he got carried away and delved into his deepest desires.

His lips were full and moist from the never-ending salivation by his moist tongue. His eyes flickered more frequently than normal as he put his thoughts into order. He took deep breaths at irregular times as his passion made him forget to breathe properly.

"...I don't know. Every time I think about it, I can't wrap my head around how a parent can disown their child like they're nothing," Pierce said and stopped talking, the silence making Rafe's attention drift back to his ears.

He seemed to have done a one-eighty and brought the conversation to the reason for his homelessness. Rafe nodded in agreement to his last statement but tried to find the words to follow up on that.

"How did you end up out here?" Pierce asked him, and Rafe mentally slapped himself for not coming up with a different subject to lighten their little rendezvous again.

He scratched his head, trying to come up with his response. "I...I ran," he found himself mumbling before he controlled his mouth.

"Huh?" Pierce grimaced, his face changing from a tender smile to a deep frown.

"I-I ran. I couldn't take it any longer. I...I felt lonely in there. Felt like I was doing something wrong twenty-four seven. I mean, sure, there was my *mumá*, who loves me, but..." he babbled before being abruptly interrupted by Pierce's groan.

"Wait a sec. You left your house because you felt lonely? You chose to be homeless because they were just...being parents?" he growled, heat visible in his face.

"I didn't—" Rafe tried to defend himself but wasn't allowed. Pierce quickened his step, clearly frustrated, and trying to bring an end to their little walk. "Pierce, wait!"

He chased after him, navigating through people, all giving him dirty looks at his attempt. The streets were now excruciatingly busy. Lunch break was on, and everyone was marching to their hotspot with clear determination.

Rafe's vision blurred. His head was moving too fast and his breath was shortening. His agitation was growing, as were its effects on him. Why was Pierce being so hard on him? He hadn't even let him explain.

He lost his footing and came crashing down on the sidewalk. He called Pierce's name one more time and people circled around him, untouched by the human disturbance. He steadied himself with two hands, focusing his eyes on the sidewalk cracks instead of the dizzying hectic amount of people surrounding him.

"Are you okay?" He saw a pair of jeans kneeling down to reveal Pierce with a concerned look on his face. That dude needed to sort out his emotional caliber.

Rafe whispered a no and rubbed his eyes, trying to clear his vision. "I have some water in my bag," he said, meaning to take it out of his rucksack, but Pierce was already pulling the strings of it and digging his hand inside to scavenge for the water bottle.

He passed the bottle to Rafe, and he took regenerating sips, closing his eyes as he did. When he opened them again, he felt a push on his back and turned his head to see Pierce sitting next to him, holding bills in his hands and waving them at Rafe.

"I thought you were fucking homeless," he growled.

"I am," Rafe murmured.

"I thought you had no fucking money. What the fuck is wrong with you, man? You leave home to live on the streets with money in your bag? Are you a psycho or something?" Pierce's voice was becoming louder, attracting some disapproving looks from passersby.

"It… It's not like that," Rafe tried to find the energy to explain, to say more, but he couldn't.

Not that he was given a chance. Pierce pushed himself up and stood tall above the still-floored Rafe.

"I'm taking these for the fucking ice cream I just bought you. Man, I can't believe I spent my money to put you in a fucking room," he huffed and walked away.

Rafe panted and looked around him trying to regain his strength and take in what had happened. That *bruto* didn't even give him a chance to explain. He just left Rafe at the mercy of himself.

Chapter 10
Pierce

Pierce pushed the door of Les Fourches open, storing away his frustration with it. He had done his best to get Rafe and his sickening existence out of his mind, but the more he thought about it, the angrier he got.

He let it all slide away, however, as he was greeted by Vance, who was hosting on the door again. He looked up and down at him, noticing his cleanliness, and it put a smile on his face. Then he took him across the bar and to a door that read 'Personnel Only'.

He found himself being led down a long corridor with several doors. A staircase to the left led to the basement, but they used the door on the right. He found himself in a room with an array of lockers, a couple of couches, a coffee table, and hangers on every possible surface.

There were paper coffee cups and napkins on the table, T-shirts and trousers crumpled on the couches, and a bunch of shoes lying all across the floor. Vance explained that the space was the staff room where he could put away his stuff until the end of his shift. He also assigned Pierce a locker that had a label stuck on it with the name 'Imogen' on it.

"That was a hostess who used to work here, but now she's off traveling the world. I'll print a label with your name on it later, but even without it, know that it's your locker and you're the only one with the combination, so anything you put in there should be more than safe," Vance explained.

Pierce nodded and unlocked the door. The contraption was too narrow to fit his suitcase, but it could easily fit a small wardrobe of clothes in it. One problem sorted at least. He didn't have to carry his clothes with him. He could just leave them in his locker and wash them when they got dirty or smelly.

Vance let him put away his things, meaning Pierce had to part not only with his new coat but his suitcase too, which he placed behind one of the couches, hiding it from immediate view. He had not let it out of his sight in months, so he was reluctant to do so now, but Vance was waiting at the door to give him a tour of the facilities, and Pierce was forced to let go.

Vance showed him to the cellar, where all the pump beer was, and to the stock room where all the liquors were stored. He was taken through the kitchen where he was briefly introduced to the chefs at work — their names going in one ear and out the other — and to the patio on the back, decorated by colorful flowers. Finally the tour ended behind the bar where Vance went through the job with Pierce. It was three p.m. so the place was relatively empty before the after-work rush at five, as Vance explained, so that gave them plenty of time to go through the basics.

"So the register is pretty straight forward. Everything is listed in their section. So you have beer in one button, wine in another, food is separated in appetizers, mains, desserts, and sides, and cocktails have their own separate section," Vance explained, navigating through the touch screen register.

Pierce squinted. "I don't know how to make cocktails," he said with a low voice that sounded almost like a whisper.

Vance laughed and turned to meet Pierce's eyes. "Of course you don't. But you'll learn, with time. For now, if any cocktails come through, I'll make them with you. Which brings me to my next point. This little machine here," he said tapping a small black printer, "is your best friend from now on. It will print all tickets from the floor saying what the patrons want to drink and what table they're meant for. You put each table's drinks on one tray, if not more, even if it is just one drink. Let the waiters deal with them, but if you put them in one tray you might confuse them. No, scrap the might. You *will* confuse them.

"Moving on, everything behind the bar needs to remain clean at all times. And that's not just because the health inspector can bust my ass if it's not, but also because I'm OCD. and I cannot stand sticky surfaces. *Capisce*?"

Vance stared at Pierce with an intense face that cracked a smile when Pierce nodded humbly.

"I promise, I'm not a horrible person. Just—" He took a moment, thinking. Then turned to the barman at the other end. "Hey, Hollister, how would you describe me?"

Hollister folded a cloth four times and set it down under the bar, turning his head and attention to his boss. "A cranky ol' faggot," he said with a big sigh.

"Hey," Vance exclaimed. "I'm not fucking

old." He laughed it off, turning back to Pierce. "So yeah, cranky ol' faggot will do, I guess. The point is I like things a certain way. If you do those things, we'll get along just fine. If not—"

"I get the boot," Pierce interrupted.

Vance shook his head, laughing. "No, you will be a subject to my verbal abuse, which goes a bit like this," he said and turned back to Hollister. "Yo' mother-f-ucker, are you gonna wipe that melted ice, or are we gonna turn this place into a water bar?"

Hollister stopped his conversation with a patron sitting on the other side and gave Vance the finger. He used the other hand to wipe the area that his boss was talking about, and looking at the patron, replied to Vance. "Yes, I can finally wear my wetsuit then, dick."

He resumed conversation with the patron, an older, grayer guy in a suit, who chuckled at Hollister's comment.

Pierce laughed. This place was more alien than it had initially looked. It felt like this expensive, uptight restaurant would be inhabited by snobs, yet they'd given Pierce a job, and the staff harassed each other for fun. An alien world, indeed.

"So, yeah, that's my kind of harassment," Vance explained and went through a few more things with him. Finally, they ended up reading the food menu together before the clock struck four p.m.

"There's no meat anywhere on this list," Pierce commented, curious as to why.

Vance slapped his hand on the bar and put his other on his waist. "Pierce Callahan, I've been going through the entire job for an hour now, and I haven't yet mentioned once that we're a vegetarian-slash-vegan restaurant? Fuck me, I *am* getting old." He rolled his eyes at himself and Pierce laughed.

"That's so cool, man. I'm vegan. Or was. Before. You know," Pierce told him, thinking back to the same noon, and him talking to Rafe about it. Funny thing, coincidences.

"Awesome. Then you'll definitely enjoy the food here. Almost everything on the list is available as a vegan option." Vance raised his chest a bit.

Pierce shook his head. "I don't think I can afford these prices".

Vance chortled. "Staff eats free, you idiot Boy, you really are inexperienced," Vance exclaimed.

You don't even know half of it, Pierce thought. "That's amazing."

Chapter 11
Rafe

od! Get away from me, you sicko," the driver said, putting his car in slow motion and stopping at the next rentboy.

Rafe couldn't blame him. Ever since yesterday, when he fell on the ground, he had gotten so sick it was killing him. He imagined he caught something off the dirty sidewalk that made him ill, because he was feverish, his back constantly running cold sweat. His face, he'd seen in a rearview mirror of a parked car, was pale, and black circles had formed under his eyes.

He needed a place to stay. He couldn't

stay out on the streets. He would surely die, and he didn't know if anyone would care enough to remove his body from wherever it was found. The subway would probably make him worse, infested with more bacteria than a quarantined ICU. His only option was sleeping with a guy, but who would pick a sickly boy to sleep with without thinking he was going to pass on whatever he had? He couldn't spend any more money on a hostel. If he did, the meds he so desperately needed and the lack of which had brought him to his current state would be even further away from his grasp than they were originally. He needed to make money quick. He needed to get better even quicker. And it was such crap that one relied upon the other to happen.

That guy had been the fourth person to reject him, and with every no, his knees gave way a bit more to the gravity pulling them down. He decided to reach out to some of the other boys on the street. He walked car by car, supporting himself on their surfaces, and reached the nearest boy. He was not much older than Rafe, but he was wearing a cap, a black chiffon top, and ripped jeans. He was also chewing gum.

"Excuse me, dude," Rafe called out to him, and seeing him, the guy stepped backward, putting his arms in between them.

"Hey, dude, don't come any closer. I don't want whatever it is you've got," he screeched, his face a disgusted mask of porcelain. The guy was wearing foundation.

Rafe nodded. "Okay, sorry. Just wanted to ask you if you know any hospitals that help homeless people," he said, his voice wavering to obscurity at points.

"Nah, I'm not homeless. I wouldn't know," he replied, chewing his gum with much more confidence now that he didn't feel threatened by Rafe.

Rafe walked away, back onto the main street, trying to desperately come up with a solution to his problem. He sat down on a step of a landing and looked around, forcing his brain to work to his advantage and not against him. He'd been around, talked to people about shelters and all that crap. Why couldn't he remember any of it? The only place that was coming to his mind was the bed he had left behind in Queens. The sweet comfort of his bedroom, surrounded by all his things. And the warmth of his *madre*'s hands rubbing the Vaporub on his chest and making her *caldo de pollo*, both to get him better in no time. And it always worked. Because the amount of love she'd put into it would be enough to replace all the drugs in the world. But that haven was no longer accessible. Not to him. Even though the room stayed vacant and his mom's heart full of affection for her only child.

He opened his eyes only to be hit by blurs. The sky was darker and the streets less busy. He'd passed out, not sure for how long, but he was certain he had. He felt disoriented. For a second, he'd even forgotten where he was.

Harlem. A little over a half hour from his house in Queens, if he took a cab. He didn't want to. He didn't want to face his *padre* or the consequences his *madre* would suffer for wanting to take him in, but he also needed her. He needed her desperately. He didn't want to die. He didn't want to break his mother's heart by leaving her alone in this world.

The need to see his mother, to survive, to get better, won over stubbornness and fear. He hailed a cab and gave the driver his destination before passing out on the backseat again.

A blinding light woke him and an angry voice penetrated his ears. "Hey, wake up. We're here."

Rafe rubbed his eyes and inspected his surroundings. Only two doors down was the blue door with number forty-six. The door to his house. Only two doors down was the sanctity of motherhood and the safety of his bedroom.

He looked at the driver, who was checking

him out with an aggressive frown. He certainly thought Rafe was a druggie that had overdosed. He was sure of it. He tried to compose himself as much as his illness and the ache in his bones allowed him and went through the notes in his rucksack. Hopefully, he'd make the money back in no time. As soon as his *mamá*'s *caldo de pollo* and love healed him.

He threw the notes at the driver and exited the vehicle.

He stumbled to the door of his house and buzzed the communicator that read 'Arena-Santos'. He waited, leaning his whole body on the wooden frame of the door and dumbing down all his other senses to focus on his hearing. He was trying to predict the chances they would answer, the chances they were both at work, or the chances that both were inside, and how they would react to being visited by their sick son.

"Hello?" came a cracked voice from the communicator, and he recognized his *mamá*, his protectress, and it gave him chills. It felt like he had called her on the phone like he did every day of the week, only this time she was finally going to get a reply.

And Rafe was prepared to give it, but he paused. He chickened out. He opened his mouth, but no words were forming. His head pulsed and his temples pushed inwards, reminding him that he didn't have much choice in the matter. If he wanted to live, he had to talk.

"*Mamá*," he croaked, "it's me."

She didn't reply. A click was heard and then the communicator's white noise deafened his ear, giving him no other sounds until the entrance door opened and his *madre*, in a dressing gown with a mix of panic and fear in her face, appeared. She moaned when she took him in her arms and put his head on her chest.

"*Que pasó*, Rafael? What's wrong?" she asked him with her distinct, flavored accent.

Rafe struggled to make his words audible when he said: "I'm sick, *mamá*. I'm—" he coughed and continued, "help me. Please."

"*Dios mio, mi chulo*, come inside," she wailed and helped him up a flight of stairs to the second floor.

She pushed number four open, and Rafe was attacked by a multitude of emotions and memories residing in his humble house.

She immediately put him on the couch and rushed in the kitchen, where Rafe could hear cupboards banging open and shut already. His mother was at work. A healer prepared to save a life. A *bruja* concocting potions to cure her precious son. Rafe couldn't stand the warmth that encompassed him. It made him feel as much alive as at peace, and his eyes felt heavy until it was a struggle to even try to keep them open.

Cayenne and cumin mixed with the smell of cooked chicken invaded his nostrils, waking him from his deep slumber. When he opened his eyes, his throat felt coarse and his brain fuzzy. He felt as if he'd been sleeping by a fireplace for hours, but there was no heat anywhere close to him, and the hours turned out to be minutes. His mother sat beside his legs, holding a red bowl. Steam wafted up from it, making the room look wavy with heat.

"*Mamacita*." He pronounced it with difficulty, a scratch in his throat preventing a clearer diction.

She shushed him, massaging his feet with the gentle fingers of one hand. "Here, drink this, baby." She passed him the red bowl, and he sat up on the couch and sipped the hot soup.

He felt its therapeutic elements going to work at once. His fever didn't bother him as much after a gulp, and his throat cleared after a few more. He could feel the color returning to his face as the fever backtracked, giving him some rest, finally.

"Just like I remember it, *mamacita*," he commented with a satisfactory smile on his face.

"What's going on, Rafael? Why are you so sick?" she asked him, her voice wavering, off-key.

"I think I caught something yesterday when I fell on the street. And since I'm not on my meds, it is much worse than for a normal, healthy person," he told her, stressing everything that wasn't right with him. Her eyes looked away and to the floor at his explanation.

When he realized she wasn't going to give him anything, he asked. "Where is *papá*?"

"Work. He's doing night shifts this week," she replied.

Rafe murmured to himself. "So we got another five to six hours to stay."

His mother snapped her eyes back to her son, looking annoyed. "You will stay for as long as you want. I'm not going to let him kick his sick son out on the streets," she said.

Rafe smiled broadly. His gaze, however, was not set on his *mamá* anymore but the blanket she had covered him with. He was going to make it after all. He was a lucky—and poor, surely—bastard. While he was in a daze between sleep and consciousness, she put a thermometer in his mouth, and he held it there with his teeth. Then seconds later, she was rubbing Vaporub on his chest. Just before he passed out, he saw his mother take the thermometer and check it with a satisfied smile on her face.

Yep, he was going to be just fine.

***

He awoke to the abrupt, heaving voice of his *padre* shouting in his ear, and before he could react in any sort of way, his forearm was crushed by his *padre*'s arm as he pulled him from under the blanket and forced him on his feet, bringing a definite end to his rest.

In an instant, he was washed with the clear image of his *padre*. Past memories washed his brain anew. His salt-and-pepper facial hair as aggressive as the wrinkles at the corners of his eyes. His mustache a heavy coat on his top lip. And of course, nothing beat the memory of his *papá*'s assaulting voice that echoed through walls, stone or paper-thin.

"But Andreas, he's sick," his *mamacita* begged, pulling at his sleeve.

He jerked his head towards her and his eyes did the talking before any of the words. "*Cállate*, Eva. I will not have *un anómalo* in my house, infesting it with his disease. Especially one who is unappreciative of all I've offered him, changing his crapped-up pants, paying to put a roof over his head and some clothes on his back and bread on the table, and who's wasted all my money on being *un artista. Un homosexual. Una basura.* Let him get what's coming to him," he said, spitting out the words as he uttered them.

"*Basura, padre? Basura?* So all this time you've been paying for my crap, have I meant nothing to you? Am I just trash now? Is your dying son *una basura*?"

His *padre* didn't reply. Instead, he hurled forward, raising his arm above him and bringing it down with force on the side of Rafe's head. Rafe's knees wavered, but he stood his ground as the person who had given life to him assaulted him with words as much as actions. Rafe's eyes instinctively turned to his *madre*. She was standing still, a few feet behind his *padre*, looking passively at the scene, hand covering her mouth as if she couldn't take in the view.

"You—you said you wouldn't let him do this to me again. Not this time," Rafe stuttered, the force of his *padre*'s strikes making his voice falter, and his hands attempting to create a shield between them.

His *madre* looked him straight in the eye when she gave her reply. "Maybe if you listened to your *papá,* Rafael, things would get better for you."

Rafe wailed when his dad slapped him in the ear so hard all he could hear was a whistling noise.

"Andreas!" his *mamá* snapped at her husband.

He exhaled and planted a slap in her cheek,

then turned back to Rafe and grabbed him by his shirt, lifting it up and pushing him towards the door.

"Come back here when you've become *un hombre* again. I won't have your sickness in this house, *maricón*." He opened the door and continued forcing him out of the way, down the stairs, his *mamá* following close behind.

"*Tu no eres mi padre, pendejo*," Rafe cursed when they finally reached the main door and the young man was reunited with the winter weather.

"And you are not my son," he replied.

Rafe's eyes reddened. He hadn't meant what he said when he did—he had only been trying to pull some humanity out of him, some of the paternity that he was hiding deep, deep down inside. He didn't anticipate his *padre* disowning him, but it made sense when it happened. Everything fell into place.

The years of his *madre*'s abuse. The years of his bullying. The years of constant judgment, criticism, inadequacy. The everlasting feelings of uncertainty. The neverending sense of danger. The unpredictability of the threat. The strikes. The punches. The kicks. The broken walls. The broken furniture. The broken dreams. The loneliness. The depression. The need.

And it all made sense. Now, it did. Andreas

Arena Soto was not his *padre*. He was a stranger. A murderer. A murderer of innocence.

His *madre* gave him his rucksack.

"You promised," he told her.

She didn't dare look him in the eyes. She looked away, drawn back inside by Andreas. And that's how Rafe came into another realization that night.

For all the years of his bullying, she was there but not really there. All the judgment, the criticism, the inadequacy, she reinforced. The everlasting feelings of uncertainty? They were there because of her. The never-ending sense of danger? Was due to her inaction. Andreas Arena Soto wasn't his father; he was a stranger. But Eva Santos Juarez was also not his *madre*. She was a perpetrator. And that realization hurt more than anything else.

He took a good last look at the blue door and waved goodbye to his old family. Now he was on his own, and despite his hurt, now it didn't look like such a bad option. He climbed down the steps and walked. He felt so much better now. Thankfully. So he walked. He walked all night.

Chapter 12
Pierce

Pierce settled the pint glass on the beer mat and looked the patron in the eyes, his icy, blue eyes, and told him, "That's five bucks, buddy."

The guy, a man in his late twenties in a navy blue suit with blonde hair and a million dollar smile, put another note on the pile next to his beer. For all Pierce knew, he *was* worth a million dollars. That was the kind of clientele his bar attracted. Perhaps not millionaires per se, but people with dough, for sure.

It was a Thursday night. It was quiet, which worried Pierce, as he relied so much on making good tips on his work days, if he was to ever get off the streets. Not that he was unappreciative. He was grateful and thankful to finally have something to hold on to. It'd only been two weeks since he started working in Les Fourches, and he'd already managed to put three hundred dollars to the side, in a small pocket in his suitcase, for his future home. Or room, more likely. There were times that he got carried away and thought he could actually make more than enough to rent an apartment to himself, but whenever he'd look at the prices around town, he'd be stomped back to reality.

He only worked weekends. Fridays and Saturdays and sometimes, like today, Thursdays. He'd done six shifts so far, excluding his training day, and Vance was very pleased with him. He'd helped him set up a bank account so that he could get some of his wages deposited in there, to build his credit and help in his search for a room—which would start, from the looks of it, in a few weeks' time. He had also worked a shift with him the past week, which Pierce had worried about at first, but then he'd realized how much fun Vance actually was to work with and had enjoyed a good and bountiful workday.

He'd also dragged Pierce along with him one afternoon for shopping. They went to several clothing stores and shopped for clothes for work. Pierce didn't want to spend any money, especially on such expensive places, but seeing the radiant smile on his boss's face and the pile of money in his pocket, he succumbed to the temptation and decide to try a few shirts. In the end, Vance paid for half his things anyway, which made Pierce's heart warm up.

He still didn't know how he'd gotten so lucky to have found not only a job but one working for a great guy who treated his staff with so much respect. Every single one of his colleagues had nothing bad or mean to say about Vance, unless it was to his face, in which case they went all wild with punchlines.

He had found out that there weren't as many people working at the bar as he had initially thought. There were three weekday waitresses and a waiter, three extra guys for the busy weekend, two full-time bartenders, and Pierce and Vance. He didn't include the kitchen because he hardly ever interacted with them. It was nothing personal; they just always seemed to leave straight after their shifts. The majority of the staff was indeed men— and handsome ones at that, it being a primarily gay area, frequented by the likes of homos, queens, fag hags, lesbos, and businessmen and women.

Pierce had grown a new habit of having a sneaky beer or two after work. He'd only made the mistake of chugging once and then had to deal with the consequences of a hangover the day after. It had reminded him, however, how much he loved being healthy, which didn't include the consumption of alcohol. Drinking was technically illegal for him anyway, but everyone turned a blind eye, as it happened.

With the ability to finally afford his daily meals, he had returned to a vegan diet, helped by the fact that his workplace, among all the other awesome things it did for him, had some fantastic food. Even being back on his beloved diet for little under a week, he found his energy levels returning to superb and his consciousness clearing up, making up for the time he'd spend not being a strict vegetarian. He also wished he could go back to the gym, but that would remain an unfulfilled wish for a lot longer. He did some crunches at work, but other than that he wasn't really able to do much.

For all the good things in his life, he still didn't have a warm bed to sleep in every night. He hadn't told anyone he worked with his status, and he had asked Vance to not spill any beans either, even though he thought that someone might have a spare bed or couch to help him out. He liked his colleagues, but he didn't want to wear out his relationship with them before it had even started. So he'd resolved to sleeping in the subway, since the streets were getting too cold for roaming in the middle of the night, let alone sleeping.

"Can I get the lentil quinoa burger with a portion of fries?" the handsome guy asked Pierce, looking up from the menu and setting it down as Pierce put the order through to the kitchen.

"Done. Can I get ya anything else?" Pierce asked.

The guy shook his head. Pierce started to move to the other side of the bar, but the guy interrupted.

"Take a break, man. There's nothing to do," he told him.

Pierce looked at him and smiled with a chuckle. He still hadn't grown used to talking to people at the bar, like a good barman was meant for. He decided to give it a shot. He went back to the guy and his fingers grabbed his end of the bar.

"So, you come here often?" he asked, and he gritted his teeth to keep from rolling his eyes, which he didn't want to do in front of the patron and embarrass himself more.

To his surprise, the guy answered in a genuine and friendly tone. "Quite often."

"Cool," was all Pierce managed to comment to the guy's reply. Now what did he say? "You like it here?"

The guy nodded. "It's got the best food

in town. And good eye candy too." The guy didn't even blush for saying that. Pierce, on the other hand, did. "I'm just messing with you. I'm Damian." He stretched his hand out over the bar, and Pierce had no other choice but to shake it. He let the shake linger for a lot longer than usual before he let go.

The food was ready and Pierce checked the lift on the back bar where the man's food was waiting. Pierce served it to Damian and let him eat in quiet, reaching the other end of the bar as another patron graced him with his presence. He was thankful for that. He didn't know how to respond to advances. It wasn't that he didn't like the guy, but it just felt wrong, being touched by Damian.

"A Coors Light, please," said the new customer, a much older guy, and straight from the looks of it. They didn't have those very often in here.

Pierce popped a bottle open for him and took the guy's money as he noticed a kid walking down the street outside. His hair was shaved short and raven black, and he was short and skinny, with a tank top on that fell well over his knees. He froze for a moment. The boy looked so much like Rafe, he felt the need to run outside and catch up with him. But it wasn't him. A simple turn of the head had proved as much.

Rafe. Pierce still couldn't shake the guilt for how he'd treated Rafe. He hadn't even let him explain himself. Not that he needed to explain anything to anyone. Pierce had acted like a dick. Like a judge, jury, and executioner of all things that didn't agree with his morals or beliefs. He was constantly slapping himself for how out of line he had gone. Even going as far as to take Rafe's money from his bag and leaving him there, on the ground, helpless.

"Argh!" he growled as he opened the register to get change, and his two bar friends jerked their attention to him. "Sorry, guys. Just—not enough change in the register." He excused himself and gave the older guy his change.

For the rest of the evening, Pierce's eye would train outside, looking for the boy he had wronged. But he wasn't anywhere around. He knew that. He knew Rafe didn't venture as far down as the Village, although he had no idea why. If there was anywhere for a gay boy like him to be, that was the Village. He might even be able to find a job just like Pierce had.

The clock struck eight, and the bar filled with patrons ready to grab their dinner or evening drink with friends. Another guy was supposed to be working with him tonight but had called in sick, so Pierce was willing to see how he would handle a busy night on his own. What drove him was the amount of tips at the end of the night, which he wouldn't have to share with anyone else except the waiters.

So he worked. And the more he worked, the more Rafe traveled out of his mind. Occasionally between orders, he would look at the door, as if he was waiting for Rafe, but they hadn't arranged to meet. They probably wouldn't see each other again.

At the end of the night, there were only four people in Les Fourches: Pierce, Vance, Katie — a waitress — and Damian, the white collar gay that hadn't stopped ordering and flirting with Pierce. The guy had probably consumed more than ten glasses of beer in between his snacks and food orders. He was still fine. Pierce had never seen anyone handle his drink so masterfully.

"Hey, Damian, I'm afraid we'll have to close your tab now," Pierce told him, distracting him from browsing his smartphone.

He looked up at Pierce and smiled. "Of course. Yes. How much do I owe ya?"

Pierce set down a check, quoting it. "It's eighty-seven ninety nine," he said. He couldn't understand how people spent so much on drinks when he barely had a dime in his pocket on most days. He couldn't understand how much they had to make to be able to spend almost a hundred bucks every day.

Damian counted the bills next to his beer mat, and although it was the right amount, he sent his hand digging on the inside pocket of his suit and pulled out another thirty dollars, then gave everything to Pierce. Adding this tip to the pile, he had made a little over two hundred dollars in one night.

In the end, on nights like these, he didn't care how people made money and how they spent it if they were being generous enough to share some of that in gratitude of his service.

He folded it and put it in his front pocket, reminding himself to add it to his savings in his suitcase.

"So, Pierce, what are you doing later?" Damian asked from his position, and Vance and Katie, who were both counting money at the other end, looked up with naughty smiles on their faces.

What was he doing later? He was going back to his hostel and crashing hard on his mattress before tomorrow's long shift, trying not to think how much he'd wronged Rafe. But he couldn't say that, could he?

"I don't know. Not much," he replied, leaving it ambiguous. He wasn't stupid. He had been flirted with before, and he had flirted before. He wasn't as cruelly clueless as his colleagues thought he was. He just didn't feel like doing these things at work.

"Did you wanna watch a movie on Netflix at my place?" Pierce gave the finger to the sniggers that arrived almost on cue from the other side of the bar and smiled at Damian. A night in a proper house with a beautiful man like him didn't sound so bad. And they all knew what "Netflix at my place" meant, which again didn't sound as terrible to Pierce as another night in the hostel.

"Sure," he said, and Damian got up and exited the building, telling him he'd wait outside.

Pierce looked over to his boss. "Can I go now?"

Vance chuckled but struggled to contain himself, so what came out of his mouth was a fine marriage between cackle and shriek. "Yes. Go. Watch 'Netflix' with your 'friend.' Keep it family friendly." Pierce shot a menacing glance at him. "The list, I mean. Don't go for anything too saucy," he finished with a far more composed voice, which broke into loud laughter in the end.

Pierce shrugged him off and went to the staff room, put his money in the suitcase, and carried it outside to meet Damian.

They took a cab to Brooklyn, and as they crossed the Williamsburg Bridge, Pierce left his stress and worries in Manhattan. He'd never ventured off the island since he'd gotten to the

City, and he wasn't familiar with the transportation system. But he brushed everything off. If it came to it, he'd take another cab. He'd find a solution. At the moment, he needed Damian's company, and he would take all he could from it.

Damian, as it turned out, lived in an apartment complex not more than ten floors in height. He lived on the ninth, in a studio flat, unlike his image. His clothes screamed "I've got money and I ain't afraid to use it," but his house screamed — no, more like whispered, "Welcome to my humble abode." It was a simple place with pastel yellow walls, a couple of sofas, a small TV, books, magazines, and everything in between thrown everywhere and a kitchen that seemed eager to be more uptight but whose anime inhabitants begged to differ. There was everything from *Pokémon* mugs to *Attack on Titan* cutting boards and *Minecraft* fridge magnets. Damian was a super geek, and he hid it very well.

Damian rushed to tidy the living room up while Pierce took a tour of the house and used the bathroom. When he returned to the main room, Damian was sitting down on the sofa in his pajamas, holding a remote, and the TV was tuned to Netflix.

"I thought you were kidding about watching Netflix," Pierce grinned.

Damian laughed. "Well, the night is still young, and I need to catch up on *Once Upon A Time*," he responded and put his show on as Pierce took seat next to him. "You can take your shoes off if you want. Feel at home."

Pierce did take his shoes off, and thank the divinities that he had bought new socks and actually *worn* them to work, or Damian would have been introduced to skanky, rugged Mr. Sock and its holes.

For the next forty minutes, Damian's only words were a commentary accompaniment with the new episode, a show Pierce had never watched. He *did* try to share Damian's excitement, but half the time he didn't know what was happening and the other half what the characters were talking about. So he kept quiet and waited for the episode to finish.

Damian poured them some wine. He didn't know how that man could still drink after so many beers and how he could still be awake. Pierce's own eyes were feeling heavier by the minute. But that was when things got interesting, and all his senses—and some parts—fully awoke.

Damian had put a slow song on and took a seat next to Pierce, grabbing his cock fervently, surprising Pierce. Next, he dug his face into his and kissed him with passion, his tongue fighting with Pierce's. Pierce let Damian use him as he pleased, stretching his hands to his side and relaxing his body in its position. But Damian seemed eager to juice Pierce out before doing anything else.

And just when Pierce got comfortable in Damian's arms and everything seemed as many miles away as they actually were when he closed his eyes, Rafe's affectionate smile attacked him, standing still in front of him, laughing, or simply staring.

Pierce flicked his eyes wide open and looked at Damian's rich eyelids, envisioning something completely different in the darkness. Pierce focused his gaze on him.

Damian started on the neck and pulled Pierce's shirt off before he moved to his nipples. Pierce followed his every step, bringing his mind's attention to the handsome man adoring his body. But with every step that brought Damian closer to Pierce's crotch, his face was replaced with Rafe's dark features, his full lips kissing his abs, his eyes looking back at Pierce, ensuring he was doing everything right.

Damian/Rafe unzipped Pierce's jeans, and Pierce felt the pang of guilt down on his chest. He pushed Damian up and told him he couldn't. Damian didn't look offended, only curious.

"I...I just don't want my first time to be like this," he said to him. He got up, zipped his pants, and started looking for his jacket when Damian reached for his hand.

"You're a virgin?" he asked him. His expression was apologetic, not angry.

Pierce nodded.

Damian rubbed Pierce's hand. "Aw, I'm sorry. I wouldn't have been so forward if I'd known. You're such a good kisser." He pulled Pierce back down to the sofa and put a little distance between them without letting go of his hand.

Pierce blushed. "Thanks. But it's not that. I've done things with boys before. Just never anything below the waist. I'm not holier-than-thou, only willing to give it to the only one. It's just, I'm...there's...I..." he began but didn't know how to describe Rafe's intrusion in their little session.

"There's another guy, and let me guess, he's haunting your thoughts?" Damian concluded. Pierce nodded. "I know. I've been through that crap. I understand. I just hope he's worth it. You're a fine man," he said.

Pierce shook his head. "He's better than I'll ever be," he said, even though he didn't know where it'd come from and how he'd come to that conclusion. He barely even knew Rafe. How was it possible he was saying things like that?

"That's adorable. You're in love," Damian replied as if reading his mind. Pierce didn't respond. "Good luck with him. I hope he doesn't torture you." Damian let go of Pierce's hand and got up. "Well, I'm beat. You can crash here if you want to."

"Really? But we didn't even—" Pierce started to say, but Damian interrupted him.

"Who do you think I am, mister? A slut? Just because we didn't do anything I'll throw you out so late in the night? Puh-lease," he said and giggled, heading off into his bedroom.

He brought a pillow and a blanket to Pierce, who embraced them both, and as soon as the lights went out, so was he.

Chapter 13
Pierce

Pierce might not have managed to get Rafe out of his mind over the next few days, but he had managed to make a new friend in Damian, who had dropped by Les Fourches on both Friday and Saturday to chat with Pierce and grab some food before heading off to dates.

"I want to find a guy to torture my own thoughts and dreams," Damian told him before heading out, leaving behind a ten dollar tip.

Despite Pierce's repeated insistence that nothing had happened between the two of them, almost the entire staff were in on the joke that Vance himself had started about Pierce having found a boyfriend.

"He's a really good guy, Vance, but I'm not ," Pierce told Vance for the millionth time. "Maybe *you* are. Word of caution, though. He's a real geek."

"I love me a good geek," was his reply as he set off to show a new arrival to their table.

"I'll set it up," Pierce shouted his way, turning a few heads his way. "What?" he told the people looking at him.

The next day, Sunday, he was off work until the next weekend, so after waking up and checking out of the hostel later than usual, he decided to take a walk to one of the restaurants around the accommodation. He had changed hostels since he'd got a job and had found something even cheaper now that he had access to the internet and set dates. He had kept true to his word and only stayed in one the day before his shift until the day after. Usually a three-night stay cost him a hundred dollars. He was okay with the arrangement since he was slowly building up his funds to find his own place. The next hostel was only a street away from where he'd saved Rafe.

Not that he had seen Rafe. He assumed he was staying away from a place he considered dangerous. Not only had he been attacked by a gang, but by a homeless dude who had played nice and then treated him like a dickhead in the end.

He found his new favorite local restaurant and took a seat inside, ordering a soda and some bread for starters. He kept looking out the window, unwilling to lose hope at the chance to meet Rafe. He ended up ordering mushroom and lentil soup and french fries. A cringe-worthy combo, perhaps, but one he'd been craving since the night before.

When he was all paid up, he went out and the sky was dark. It was already seven p.m., and with clocks going backward a week ago, it looked much later than it felt. He didn't know where he was going tonight. The weather was not as chilly as the other nights, but why would he ever sleep outside when he had the moderate warmth of the subway? He knew where the closest station was and made his way toward it, cutting through a street he hadn't before.

It was dark and quiet, a lot of cars driving by in slow motion. The further down he walked, he saw there were a lot of people standing on both sides of the street. They were all young men. He had, accidentally, found a cruising place. He tried not to stare, but the more gazes he felt on him, the more he felt inclined to look back. Some even howled at him, trying to get picked up. Even if he did want one, what would he possibly say? "I have this cozy train on the 3-Line we can use"?

A car slowed down, and he heard a familiar voice. His eyes traced it, and his legs took him closer.

"I'm *very* good with whips," Rafe said to the driver of a crimson Volkswagen. "If that's what you're into," he added.

He didn't sound normal. Not like the sweet Rafe he'd talked to. He sounded passionate and sexy. He sounded dirty.

"Rafe?" he called to him.

Rafe turned his head and saw Pierce. His eyes grew wide. "What are you doing here?"

"I was going to ask you the same thing. Are you actually selling yourself to a stranger?" Pierce said before he could stop himself, realizing how accusatory he had sounded.

"What it's got to do with you if I do?" Rafe asked.

Pierce got closer. He was only a few feet from Rafe, now. "Nothing, I know. But how can you trust that all these people don't have AIDS or something? How can you trust they're not ax murderers?" Pierce pleaded with Rafe.

"Hey! I'm just a teacher, dude," the guy from inside the car said.

"Yeah, have you heard of Grindr, *dude*?" Pierce replied, turning his attention back to Rafe.

Rafe had already opened the door to the car. "Let me get this straight, Pierce. You have no right to judge me. You have no right to control me. I don't know you, and *you* don't know *me*. So do us both a favor and get the fuck out of here. You're polluting everyone with your crappy energy," he said and got in the car. "Drive," he told the teacher, and the red Volkswagen veered off, leaving Pierce alone with a bunch of rentboys staring at him.

He shook off the tears he wasn't aware were threatening his eyes and resumed his journey to the subway station.

Had he hurt Rafe so bad he found the need to sell his body to survive, or had that been something he was already doing when he met him? He couldn't imagine the sweet boy sexing it up for money. Hell, he couldn't imagine him finding pleasure in any sexual endeavor. And not because he wasn't attractive but because he seemed so innocent—too innocent to be doing anything as dirty as sex with strangers.

He really wanted to talk to Rafe and explain himself, but he didn't seem as eager to do the same. Had he been such a complete tool that it had cost himself a good friend? What could he possibly do to make it up to him?

What was he supposed to do until next Friday, when his next shift was? Thinking of the week ahead, he already felt lonely. Sure, he could swing by his work and have a drink, but why spend money and delay his apartment hunt? And then, he thought, what was the point of saving to find a room to rent if he had no one to invite, no one to share its warmth with?

How he missed home. He might not have been accepted for who he was there, but he had friends that visited him and did things together, or he always had his mother to cook with, which was a fun activity, even though she thought being vegan was Satan clawing his way to Pierce's soul.

He saw a phone booth, and the longing to call home clawed in his heart just like his veganism had supposedly, and he found himself dialing home in no time.

"Hello!" came the answer from who other than his mom.

"Hi, Mom," he told her.

There was a deafening pause for a few seconds.

"Why are you calling, Pierce? Did you decide to atone for your sins and claim the Heavenly Father as your Lord and Savior again?"

Pierce rolled his eyes. "No," he told her, "I called to tell you that I found a job last month and soon I'll be able to afford a room to live in."

Another long pause. He was trying to

determine whether the pause was a delay in the line, or his mother thinking what insult to throw next. "Pierce, you know you always have a home here, with your father and I. All you have to do is ask for forgiveness and stop…sinning," she said with her shrill voice. A voice that actually had the ability to turn Pierce into the devil his mother was so afraid of.

"I can't believe your *homeless* son is calling you after six months and that's all you have to tell him," he asked maintaining his calm. For now.

She exhaled with attitude. The attitude that said, *Oh, Pierce, you're so young and, you know nothing.*

"I cannot give up my place in Heaven because my son has decided to," she said in a calm manner. "I don't know what kind of people you've met to have made you this way, but I can't have you sinning under my roof."

He could picture her in his head. The way she would smile gently. The way her eyes would squint and her cheeks would ball up, forming a fake tenderness that could send Pierce ballistic.

"Go fuck yourself," he said, and slammed the phone back on the receiver. There were a million things he wanted to tell her. But that seemed to sum everything up. She was not a mother. She was a puppet. And he didn't know if puppets had the ability to acquire knowledge or even listen.

He paid the fare for the subway and sat down in an almost empty train. He took his book out of his suitcase and started reading, trying not to think of innocence lost and of devilish mothers finding salvation. It was going to be a long night. Thank goodness it was a long book.

Chapter 14
Rafe

he next day, Rafe couldn't get Pierce out of his mind. Not that he had been able to while whipping and tying up the naughty teacher that had picked him up. He didn't do kink, but for the extra cash he had charged him, he wouldn't mind adding it to his services. One-twenty for a night was more than he'd made since he started in this dangerous profession.

He subconsciously went through all the places he'd met Pierce. He walked through Central Park and then the cafe he'd taken him after the attack. When he realized he was standing at the very alley the *cholos* had pulled him down, he accepted the fact that he wasn't ready to let Pierce go so easily. He went to the hostel where he knew Pierce preferred to stay and asked if he had been around, but they told him he hadn't turned up in weeks. Rafe was worried. He wished he had asked where Pierce's job was so that he could check there as well, if he still worked there.

He met Marissa for their customary hot drink and pizza slice at four. He had only found the guts to go back to Mario's and apologize to his friend a week after he had been kicked out of his family house. Marissa had taken him back in. He didn't even need to explain. She did want to go and kick his father's ass, however, when he told her what happened. They were back to besties in a matter of seconds.

When it got to five o'clock, he headed off, wanting to get an early start. The last couple of weeks he'd managed to do two clients in a few nights. With the light going out so early in the day, men got horny much earlier, and he managed to fit in an evening client before a midnighter. There had been nights when he had had no one, but he was doing well, all in all.

He got there a little before six and waited for the guys to start driving by. At half past six, an old man in a Porsche stopped in front of Rafe, and he was already calculating how much to raise his price for such a…prestigious man.

"Hello, sexy. What's your name?" Rafe smiled as soon as the window had rolled down.

"Rafe, can we talk?" someone said behind him, and Rafe recognized the raspy voice. Pierce appeared from the shadows, his face pinker than he remembered it and looking at Rafe's chest rather than his eyes.

"I have nothing to say to you," Rafe snapped, biting his lip. He'd missed Pierce and his company. But he'd be damned if he let such a venomous man back in his life.

"Why are you doing this?" Pierce asked. He was now standing at the end of the sidewalk, a car away from Rafe.

Rafe shrugged. "Got to make a living somehow, don't I? Not everyone can walk into a bar and get a job." He turned to the old man again.

"Have you even tried it?" Pierce insisted. "I'm sorry, that's not what I meant."

Rafe took some steps closer to Pierce, forgetting the senior in the car. This man had the ability to infuriate him and weaken his knees at the same time. Right now, the former was winning. "What *do* you mean, Pierce?"

He took a moment before he answered. "I-I care about you," he mumbled.

Knees were about to give up on him, but

he let the infuriated part take over before he showed how easy he was. "A man who cares about someone else lets them explain why they thought leaving home was the best option for them, not judge them before they can explain why they felt that way," he hissed, not wanting to turn heads in the darkness.

"Tell me," Pierce begged. It was a little louder than a whisper. It was a plea. It was desperate.

"It's too late now." Rafe pushed the warmth in his heart deeper inside and stood strong. That man was poison for him. He couldn't let himself be sucked back in.

He turned and opened the door to the old man's car. They could discuss details on the ride back to his place. Before he managed to take the seat, a hand pulled him back gently, and Pierce closed the door.

"I'm sorry, old man, he's taken for the night," he told the driver.

"Whatever," he said and drove to the next rentboy.

Rafe protested. He was losing money. He was losing his reputation. He wanted to punch Pierce. He told him all these things.

"Rafe, I'm sorry I was such a dick. It's what happens when I open my mouth. So I'm gonna shut it and let you tell me about you, hoping you can forgive me, because frankly? I can't imagine not talking to you ever again," Pierce said and waited for Rafe's response.

Rafe couldn't believe that a guy like Pierce wanted his friendship. Pierce was poison, but if poison tasted so sweet, to hell with antidotes.

They walked down the road, taking a left and finding a Chinese restaurant to sit in. Rafe only ordered a side of spring rolls and a glass of water. Pierce ordered juice for both of them and a main course of rice noodles to share.

And finally Rafe let go of all the resentment about Pierce that had crept up in him and let the charming, toxic guy win him over with a nice dinner night. Which he'd be damned if he paid for.

Pierce told him about his job and his colleagues and how excited he was but how empty his routine was without a Rafe to save from gangs. Rafe chuckled even though it was hardly a joke and hardly funny. When he finished his brief update he gave the mic over to Rafe.

"So can you tell this idiot why you left home?"

The noodles came that very moment, giving Rafe time to think how and where to start the story. When the waitress left, he was ready. He just didn't know how ready Pierce was for it.

"My dad was always abusive. He always

bullied me. Called me names. Nothing I ever did ever pleased him. I was always bullied at school, too. I only had a couple of friends, but mainly I kept to myself, which only gave fuel to the fire. I was the school faggot, the sissy, the cocksucker. That's what they called me," he said. Pierce's eyes were glued on Rafe's, his hands crossed in front of his mouth.

"The only nice person in my life was my *mamacita*. But my dad beat her, and she couldn't do a lot for me. She tried, though. God, she tried. And then, I found someone else who liked me. Some boy in my neighborhood, who at first I thought was another, more dangerous, bully. But he turned out to be hopelessly in love with me, and you know…what else does a gay teenager with no friends and no support want? So I let him love me. He was only a year older than me and he seemed experienced, but I didn't care about these things. I cared for his kisses and his hugs. And then I let him in. I lost my virginity to him and didn't even bat an eye about it. I wanted to do it and I did it.

"But after the night we spent together at his place when his parents were out, he disappeared. I started worrying. I thought that's all he ever wanted from me. I even thought he slept with me to win a bet. Then, two weeks later, he turned up, texted me, and asked to meet up. I wasn't sure about meeting him. I thought he'd betrayed me. But I did want to find out why he'd disappeared. So I met him at his house. And he told me why. He found out he was HIV positive. And he was afraid he had passed it on to me."

Rafe paused to take a bite and inspect Pierce. He was waiting for the story to go on. He hadn't taken a single bite of the noodles or a sip of his juice.

"I went through all the exams and the crap and waited for the results. I was certain I didn't have anything. I didn't feel different. I didn't think my first time would actually screw me up so badly. But I had the fear. What if? And two weeks later the results were in, and I was positive."

Rafe, again, examined Pierce's face, who tried to show his compassion by pursing his lips and wrinkling his forehead.

"I told my parents. I didn't know how else I could afford the medication. So I had to tell them two things. That I was gay, and that I had HIV. How cliché was I?

"Turns out, a lot. My dad started beating me up. When my mom tried to stop him, he beat her up. He didn't want anything to do with my sicknesses. Both of them. He blanked me out. Didn't talk to me anymore. Just beat me up if I tried to go out. Until I got a very bad cough and I was homebound. My mother stayed home to look after me. When my dad came back she asked him for money for a cough syrup. My dad went ballistic, beating my mom, me, throwing stuff across the room. He said he'd go to hell before paying for my fix. He was crazy. He didn't know what he was talking about. And the more we tried to reason with him, the more violent he became. He broke my mom's nose. He punched me in the eye. I just knew I couldn't be in there with him anymore. I was only making things worse for my mom. So I ran. To keep my mom and myself safe," Rafe finished and took a gulp of his juice.

Pierce was silent. He didn't know what to say.

"That's my story," Rafe said.

Pierce shook his head and blinked several times. He rubbed his eyes. "Wow! So what are you doing now? Are you taking your meds?"

Rafe laughed. When other patrons turned staring at him he tried to stop but snorted like a pig.

"I'm homeless, Pierce. I'm lucky if I make fifty bucks from a fuck. And my meds cost almost two thousand. How on earth do you think I could be on my meds? I've managed to buy them a couple times, but they only last a month. I made them last two. But they don't work that way. You need them every day. Every month."

Pierce nodded. "There must be some charity or someone that helps people with HIV," he said, and Rafe snorted again.

"Yeah, and we both know what kind of charities and places New York City has. If I wait for them to help me, I'll die first," he said.

"We'll find a way. I'll help you. *I'll* find a way," Pierce said and reached for Rafe's hand across the table.

Little spiders crawled up his arm and his heart pumped louder. This man, this guy! Perhaps he wasn't as poisonous as he thought. Now if he could convince his body the same before he collapsed from all the reactions Pierce's touch caused to his skin, the night would be a dream.

Chapter 15
Pierce

From that day on, Pierce and Rafe didn't lose sight of each other again. Wherever they went, they went together. Sleeping in subway cars, next to each other, using Pierce's jacket as a makeshift blanket for them both. Using their spare change to browse the internet and to find a solution to Rafe's problem, or simply walking without purpose and talking endlessly about themselves.

Of course, Pierce wouldn't let Rafe rent his body again, something which stressed Rafe, he'd said, as he had grown so used to earning money for his meds that way. Between the two of them, they had a little over two thousand dollars and could afford one month of Rafe's medication, but they needed to find a more permanent fix to the problem.

On their second day living as conjoined twins, Rafe took him downtown to a place called Mario's Pizza where they were greeted by the smell of dough and herbs and a warm hug by the owner's wife, Sonia, who not only gave them both a wide smile but a free drink too.

"She's a really nice lady. She gives us a free slice and a drink every day," Rafe told Pierce once they were both sat down on one of the tables.

Rafe pulled a third chair to their table and kept looking at the door, waiting for his friend to arrive. Pierce couldn't believe this place even existed. He wished he'd known about it sooner, when he was starving and went days without proper food. It didn't look particularly busy either, so he was astounded to find out they were so generous with the services they provided. He wanted to do something good for Sonia and her big heart.

Five minutes later, the doorbell chimed and in walked a girl. She was short and a bit on the plus size side, wearing black clothes and dark make-up, and she took a seat between Rafe and Pierce. Rafe introduced her as Marissa.

She was a shy girl, for all her intimidating appearance, but Rafe felt at home around her, and Pierce was beginning to realize there was nothing sweeter than seeing Rafe happy. Even if it was feeble and temporary.

Soon after Marissa sat down, Sonia approached them to take their order, and Pierce had already made up his mind. Tonight's dinner was on him. Not so much for Rafe and Marissa as for Sonia and what she did for people like them.

"I want a Margherita and Marissa here wants a Pepperoni. Pierce? What are you getting?" Rafe asked and all eyes turned on him.

He coughed. "Can you make those two into full-size pizzas and make me a third vegetarian with no cheese and a BBQ base, please?" he asked her, and he felt all the eyes turn inquisitive when he had finished. "I'm paying for today," he explained.

Sonia came closer to him and grabbed his shoulder, putting her pad down. "Oh, honey, you don't have to pay here," she told him.

"I know. But I want to. Give back for what you do for Rafe and others like us," he replied.

She gave him a gentle hug and left to give the order to the kitchen at the back. Marissa drank her tea, concentrating on an empty spot across from her. Rafe, however, was staring at

Pierce, smiling like a baby.

"What?" Pierce asked. Not that he disliked the attention.

Rafe shook his head casually and took a sip from his cocoa. "Nothing," he said.

"Get a room made out of cardboard, dudes," Marissa mumbled retrieving her lips from the mug long enough to make her point and then slurped her hot cocoa.

Rafe pushed Marissa's arm and rolled his eyes. The truth was Pierce wouldn't mind getting a room with Rafe, even if it was made out of cardboard.

"That's it!" he exclaimed. "Thank you, Marissa," he said, and Rafe was back to staring at Pierce, looking for an explanation. "Why don't we find a room together? It surely beats sleeping on the subway, and I'm sure it will be easier to get help for you if we do."

Rafe nodded. Marissa let her mug down and pursed her lips in agreement. "You should definitely do that."

The pizzas arrived in no less than fifteen minutes, and everybody dug in. Rafe surprised Pierce when he asked if he could try his vegan pizza, said ironically, but after trying it, genuinely agreed on how good it tasted. Marissa munched on her pizza without much commentary other than a roll of her eyes whenever Pierce and Rafe got a bit cornier than she was used to.

Later that evening, after they'd waved goodbye to Marissa, the two walked around Times Square, letting the vibrant lights and the busy streets take away their worries and turn them into something mundane.

They were sitting on the bleachers of the Pavilion when Rafe brought the subject up of finding an apartment together. He didn't look at Pierce when he spoke but instead at the blinding billboards. It was quite dark now.

"Are you sure you want to find a place together? You know it's not going to be easy, right?"

Pierce put his hand on Rafe's knee and brought the boy's attention to him. "I know. But now we're a team, right? We'll do this together."

Rafe didn't say anything. He only stared into Pierce's eyes and nodded.

"I mean, at least we'll have a house, you know. Everything must be easier when you have a roof over your head," Pierce commented.

Rafe agreed. "Then all I'll need is a job and I can apply for Medicaid and free medication."

Pierce jumped in his seat and took hold of both of Rafe's shoulders. "See? Exactly. You've got yourself a solution. All we gotta do is find a room and then a job, and you'll be back on track with your health in no time."

Rafe didn't share in Pierce's excitement. "I guess," he shrugged.

"Rafe," Pierce shook him, "don't be so pessimistic. You'll see. Everything will be okay now."

Chapter 16
Rafe

nd there is always hot water, except for late at night, when the valve is switched off automatically, but it shouldn't be a problem. We've not had any complaints so far," the woman said.

She was short, brunette, with dark skin, wearing a black suit with blue heels that failed to make her taller, especially standing next to Pierce. She was giving them a tour of a house in the Bronx, a three-bedroom flat with no communal areas other than the kitchen and the bathroom.

"We don't care about the water in the middle of the night. The room is great. The area is…great. Can we get to paperwork?" Pierce asked, and Rafe, who was standing a little behind him, pinched his thigh.

"Sure. What we need from you is a holding deposit, two forms of ID, references from two past landlords, your bank accounts to run a credit check on your behalf, six weeks of pay stubs, and our agency fee is a hundred and thirty-nine dollars per person, which you will need to pay before we can run the check on you," she said, and Rafe already knew they were walking out.

It had been the seventh or eighth house they had viewed in the past week, and they all required the same. Even private landlords they had found through Craigslist required some form of income for the two of them and a damn credit check. Rafe was losing hope that he would ever be able to get his medication.

Even though Pierce and Rafe combined had enough money to pay for deposits and a month's rent, everyone wanted to run a credit check, and since Rafe had no account linked to his name, that was impossible. Everyone also asked for proof of work, which again, Rafe didn't have. No one was willing to risk letting an apartment without the security of future payments, and Rafe couldn't blame them. He didn't know if he'd let them stay in his place if he had one.

Pierce was not giving up. He kept phoning people up and getting viewings, thinking he could talk his way in and score them both a place.

That was what he was trying to do now. Explaining the situation, with as little detail as possible, in hopes it would change her mind.

"I mean, if you *are* working, we could technically run the check on your name and do the whole contract, but if you say you're working part-time, I don't think you'd pass the credit check," she told Pierce.

"No, he has to be in the contract too. He needs to apply for medical help. He will get worse if we don't find a place soon enough. Are you sure you can't make an exception for us?" Pierce tried to sound pleasant, but he usually sounded plain rude. God bless him, he couldn't shake off the brutal image no matter how hard he tried. But Rafe knew what hid under it: a heart of gold.

The real estate agent squinted and shook her head. "I'm sorry. It's not up to me. It's up to the system. If it runs the check and finds you are not earning enough, it will automatically fail you."

Pierce's beastly manners came to show when he cursed, taking Rafe by the hand, and dragging him out of the apartment.

"Jesus Christ! Now systems get to decide

for us. What's next? Asking a robot for permission to take a crap?" he shouted and slammed the door behind them.

Rafe put his hands on Pierce's shoulders and asked him to calm down. He found it impossible.

"Everyone is a fucking dick, seriously!" he said.

Rafe laughed. "I know. But we like dick, remember?" Pierce chuckled and rolled his eyes.

"Come on, let's grab some lunch," he responded, going down to the first floor and hailing a cab.

"Mr. Callahan, you are spoiling me," Rafe said when they got in the cab.

Pierce huffed. "I'm too pissed to walk or take the subway. The Village please," he said to the driver and they started their journey downtown.

They arrived at Les Fourches half an hour later and Vance was there to welcome them in the restaurant.

"Any luck, boys?" Pierce shook his head and Vance grimaced. "I'm sorry."

"Can we grab some lunch before I start?" Pierce asked him and Vance nodded, pointing them to a table next to him.

Rafe was starting to enjoy food at Les Fourches, something he never thought possible, considering all the meaty delicacies his mother had raised him with. He didn't know if he could ever go fully vegan like Pierce, but he didn't mind a vegetarian diet. It helped that the place made such delicious food.

Vance came to stand next to them while keeping an eye on the door for new patrons. "What did they say?"

Pierce uncovered his face and replied to his boss. "The usual. They need bank accounts, credit checks, pay stubs and crap. They said they could do the contract in my name, but the point is for Rafe to have a legal address to register for his meds. So fucked up."

Vance frowned. "Why didn't you do it, anyway?" he asked Pierce.

"Because I don't earn enough money and the system—*yes,* a fucking computer—would fail me," he responded, venting some of the anger while he was at it.

The waitress, Chloe, brought them their beers, both in mugs, since they were sitting so close to the window. Vance looked at her and clapped his hands together.

"But of course!" he exclaimed. Chloe jumped and waited for her boss's instructions.

"What the hell do you want?" she asked him, placing her hand where her heart was.

Vance gave her the bird and turned to

address Pierce. "This bitch just told me she's leaving, 'cause apparently she got a job in a radio station or some crap like that." Chloe winced and stuck her tongue out. Vance looked at Rafe. "Do you want a job as a waiter? Again, it's only part-time, but it will help you open a bank account and with your credit," he said.

Rafe smiled and nodded like a bobble head. "Really?"

"That's great," Pierce intervened, "but we'll still not make enough money for the system to approve us."

Vance turned to Pierce and smacked him on the head. Exactly how Rafe felt like doing. "You, Debbie Downer, if I pay all his tips and wages in his bank account, he should have a good credit score in no time. I can do the same with you," he said.

Rafe's smile widened. Things were actually looking up. If Vance really did hire him and gave them both a push, then they really could move into an apartment in no time. But Pierce didn't reciprocate in his enthusiasm.

"That will not work. Even if you do that, they will still need two months' pay stubs, which he doesn't have, and if we wait two months he might get sick again, plus he won't be making three times the rent to actually get approved, I think—" he paused and withdrew his eyes from

Vance and back to Rafe apologetically— "if I give you my tips to pay into my account then I can at least be a guarantor for Rafe, but I don't think we can both rent something without wasting any time," he finished and exhaled, making Rafe tear up.

Was he actually willing to do that for him? To give up his chance of finding a flat just so that Rafe could move in somewhere and get his medication? He didn't want to let him do that, but at the same time, he didn't have much of a choice. If he left his disease untreated, next time he had a fever, it might never come down. Next time, he might not make it out unscathed. When did life become so cruel? When had he become an adult required to make difficult decisions?

"Okay," he said, but not with much heart in it.

"Great," Vance said and clapped his hands. "Chloe, bitch, since you decided to leave us, you can train Rafe on the job."

"My pleasure," she said, inviting Rafe closer to her. Rafe got up and followed her to the back into the staff room where she handed him a gray apron and showed him to an empty locker where he could put his sack and the rest of his things.

When she brought him back to the front, she gave him a tablet that the waitresses used to take orders and let him follow her to her tables and watch while she did her best at explaining everything he needed to know, passing along her sage wisdom and giving the best service to her patrons.

It made Rafe forget his guilt and the sacrifice Pierce was making. What was he supposed to say to him? "Thank you"? How inadequate did that sound? He approached the bar to collect one of Chloe's drinks orders, so deep in concentration and thought that he jumped when Pierce touched his hand and leaned in closer.

"Don't be like that. I want to help, and you don't have to feel guilty about it. We'll find you a room, and I'll help pay all the extra costs, and as soon as you're on your treatment, we'll work on getting me a room, okay?" he whispered.

Rafe replied with a shy smile and a nod before picking up the tray and carrying it to table fifteen.

Chapter 17
Pierce

Vance came out from behind the curtain and cat-walked around Pierce, busting a few moves.

"No. You look like a clown," Pierce said, and when Vance took offense he added, "There's too much orange."

Vance put his hands on his waist. "It's beige," he replied with a fake French accent.

"Beige, schmeige, it schecks," Pierce retaliated by also faking an accent.

Vance pressed his cheeks under his eyes and raised an eyebrow. "Whatever that was, bury it as deep as you can," he told him and marched his way back into the changing room.

"Whatever," Pierce laughed.

His boss's voice echoed in his ears while he was changing. "So Rafe told me he is finally on his medication?"

Pierce nodded but remembered Vance couldn't see him and gave a vocal sound of approval.

"Does that mean you will finally start searching for your own place?"

"That's the plan, but that won't happen for another month at least."

The curtain was pulled back, and Vance appeared in a sailor's suit with a white jacket and trousers, navy blue lines defining the collar and the button line and seams. A scarf was tied sideways on his neck, and a light blue shirt was hiding underneath the buttoned suit. "Why so long?"

"Because I'm still helping Rafe with rent. If he worked more hours, perhaps I would be able to actually save something," he said and cocked his head to the side like a puppy, not so subtle with the hint.

"Don't look at me like that. You know I would if I could. What am I supposed to do? Fire all my staff and have you two run the place?" Vance reprimanded him, but it was too difficult to take him seriously in what he was wearing.

"Hm, doesn't sound that bad," Pierce

joked. "Speaking of bad, is your date—" Pierce started but was interrupted by Vance.

"Friend," he corrected.

"*Friend* who you're trying to impress by buying a new suit? Yes, *friend* is the first word that comes to mind. Is your 'friend' into sailors? 'Cause that's the only way I can imagine him liking this suit. Or is it Halloween. But Halloween is way over, so maybe you're aiming for some carnival," Pierce commented.

Vance grimaced and headed for the changing room again. "You know, I think I liked you better when I hadn't hired you yet," he said.

"Oh, you mean when I served you your face by insulting you in your own bar? Yeah, sometimes I like that Pierce better myself," he replied.

Vance's face appeared from between the curtains. "Remind me again, why did I ever hire you?"

He actually waited for the answer. Pierce tried to drag it for as long as possible, making Vance look even more ridiculous the longer he held his position like a floating, disembodied head.

"Because I'm hot and rugged, which is so obviously your type," he told him.

His boss winked at him and retreated back into his changing room. "You are right. But if you're anything to go by, I'm doomed. Unless I find a way to make all young Latinos disappear from the face of the Earth—" he started but paused as if someone had gagged him. Then his voice came across, a little louder than a whisper. "Please tell me there is no one around, because that sounded *so* wrong."

Pierce laughed out loud. Vance eventually appeared to restrain Pierce's mouth and shut him up.

"You know I can sue you for that," Pierce told him before resuming his deep laughter.

"Shut up and tell me what you think," Vance shouted at him.

Pierce opened his eyes and looked at his boss. His laughter ceased as he took him in. A grey, slim jacket hugged his upper body, matching the ashen blonde of his hair, and a pair of trousers just a tone darker lined his buttocks, thighs, and calves in a taut embrace that made Pierce feel uncomfortable.

Was it okay for his boss to turn him on? Especially when his mind was occupied by a young Latino? Pierce crossed his legs before giving Vance the thumbs up, which made him prance back into the changing room and change into his jocks.

Waiting in line to pay, Vance brought the conversation back to the initial topic. "How much have you saved for yourself so far?"

Pierce turned to his boss and gave him the pessimistic number. "A little under seven hundred. And considering it's been more than two months since I started working for you, that's bad."

"Don't say that. You've helped Rafe get healthy again. We just need to sort you out. You can't be wasting your money on hostels any longer," Vance replied as he put his hand on Pierce's back.

Pierce had never told him he slept in the subway on the weekdays and he had asked Rafe to do the same. Yes, Vance was now equally a friend and a boss, but that didn't mean he would be okay having his employees still homeless when they were on a reasonable enough income to pay for a bed, at least.

Rafe had suggested telling him because he thought Vance might even let him sleep on his couch or find someone else to host him while he was still saving, but Pierce didn't want that. He didn't want to let his colleagues know how much in need he was and change their opinion about him, or give anyone reason to think they were better than him and offer him charity. Pierce wanted to make it on his own. On his own with Rafe.

The other truth was that since Rafe and

he had joined forces, he had slept in hostels more than usual. Especially after Rafe had got the job at Les Fourches, they slept five out of seven nights in the same hostel. He didn't want to worsen Rafe's condition by adding more bacteria into his body, and if there was one place to find those, it was the subway.

Sleeping outside was no longer an option. Winter had set in in New York City, along with the Christmas decorations and the tourists from all corners of the planet. The streets were colder, noisier, and more unwelcoming than ever.

It had been a month since Rafe had gotten the job at the bar and two weeks since he'd gotten a room. Vance had worked some of his tricks when paying Rafe and even managed to give him fake pay stubs to present to potential landlords, and he was finally settled in a one-bedroom private residence in Greenpoint, Brooklyn. His landlord, Wang, lived in the bedroom, and Rafe was paying $750 a month to live in a tiny hole that fit only a bed and a canvas wardrobe that had to be moved in order to open the door. It was better than the streets, though, especially since it was warm, had a bed, and more than anything, granted him access to his drugs.

It had only been a few days since his application for help with his medication had been approved. Rafe's life had changed, and he couldn't stop thanking Pierce for it. But for Pierce, it was enough that Rafe was good and off the streets. He couldn't say the same for himself. He still had a while to go before moving into his own place.

His leg buzzed as his phone rang in his jeans. He pulled out his new phone—an old, used Nokia with limited internet capabilities—and read Rafe's name on the screen. He pressed the green button to answer.

"Hi, Pierce. How are you?"

Pierce walked outside of the store as Vance took his position in front of the register and paid up. "I'm good. Shopping with Vance for his date," he replied.

Rafe whistled. "Woo, go Vance! Anyway, that's not why I'm calling." He lowered his voice. "I just found out that Wang is going away on vacation for two weeks, and I thought you might like to crash at my place until he's back." When he finished, he remained absolutely quiet, waiting for Pierce's reply.

Pierce wanted to jump and fist-pump the air but restrained himself to a simple yes and a thank you before hanging up. It was Thursday, which meant he wouldn't have to pay for a hostel for another two weeks, and he'd get to spend more time with Rafe. It was win-win no matter what way he looked at it.

He picked up his suitcase, parted ways with Vance, and made his way for Brooklyn on the C Line. Maybe life wasn't being as unfair to him as he thought.

Chapter 18
Rafe

hen the doorbell rang, Rafe checked his hair—which had grown over the last month—to make sure nothing was pointing to the wrong direction, then opened the door.

And there he was. The guy with the suitcase. The guy with the suitcase wearing a smile on his face. And there was nothing that made Rafe happier than seeing Pierce. Pierce wiped his shoes at the doormat and entered the apartment, looking around.

"He left this morning," Rafe reassured him. "Don't worry. We're all alone." Rafe hadn't meant that as racy as it came out, but he rolled with it.

He showed Pierce into his bedroom, which he had tidied up and lit some tea candles around for some extra warmth. It was incredible how much junk one could collect in a matter of a fortnight. But once he went shopping, it was impossible to stop. He needed a bin for his trash and some more sketchbooks of varying sizes to pass his endless time between work, and, of course, a bookshelf to put said books. Before he knew it he had quite the welcoming room.

It was a rabbit hole, but it was his rabbit hole. He still had to move his wardrobe to open his bedroom door, but it was so light, it didn't really matter to him. All he wanted now was to share his sacred space with the guy who had made everything possible.

Pierce put down his suitcase and sat on the bed. "You've really worked on the place," he commented as he looked around.

"Yeah, had to do something with my time. Thank you," Rafe responded, trying to look into Pierce's eyes, but they were focused on the fairy lights he had nailed to the ceiling for extra ambience.

It was only when Rafe said thank you that Pierce turned to look at him. "I've told you to stop saying that. I promised to find a way, and I wouldn't rest until I did."

Rafe smiled. "Okay. Okay." Rafe sat next to Pierce. "Do you want to tell me what is in that suitcase?" Rafe set his eyes on the case trying to open it up with his thought. "I mean I know it belonged to your grandad, but I'm sure there's another reason why you're carrying it around, and I can't believe you still haven't told me."

Pierce didn't answer. He dragged the suitcase in front of his legs and popped it open. He took a pile of pictures out and passed them to Rafe.

"Those are all pictures my gramps took before he died. After he came out to his family and everyone turned their back on him, he took all his savings and traveled the world. Even in his sixties, he lived a full, happy life as a gay man, and he saw everything. I like to look at them. They make me feel happy. They make me dream. They give me hope that things can get better, even if I have to wait forty years for it. One day, I'd like to take pictures of my adventures like he did, but until then I have his memories. And the suitcase—he left it to me in his will. The rest of his family got nothing. He gave me this suitcase because, as it said on his letter: 'This suitcase is all I can give to my beautiful grandson and hope that it is enough.' So I like to keep both safe and sound," Pierce said while Rafe went through the photographs.

They were all so beautiful, and the first thing Rafe realized was how much Pierce looked like his grandfather. If he was going to age like him, he was going to be a charming sixty-year-old. He could see why his grandfather hadn't had a problem adjusting nicely to life as a gay man with his mature looks.

It wasn't just the looks, however. It was also the pure happiness depicted in the pictures. Not just his, but that of his friends, and surely some of them had been his lovers too. Wherever he found himself, and he had gone *everywhere*, he was surrounded by happy people. He couldn't blame Pierce for holding on to them. But he didn't like the idea that Pierce felt hopeless. He wanted to give Pierce what he had given him, but he didn't know how when he only worked two nights a week. Once he was fully on medication, he would go looking for another job, but until then he felt too weak to do so. That didn't erase his desire to get Pierce something to thank him. He was sure he'd find something. For now he would share his house, which this *bruto* had made possible, and hope it was enough.

"Want to watch a film? Wang has Netflix, so we can binge-watch 90s shows," Rafe suggested, touching Pierce's knee and getting up.

Pierce smiled. "Sure. Why not?"

Rafe exited the room and returned with a laptop in his hands. It was an expensive one. Pierce's inquisitive face was enough for Rafe to answer.

"I asked him if I can use it to send resumés and stuff. He didn't say no. So what if by stuff I meant porn and Netflix?"

Pierce's inquisitive expression remained and was joined by Pierce's laugh.

"What? I'm a man. I got needs," Rafe answered, hoping Pierce hadn't taken his joke too seriously. Sure, he did like watching porn, but he didn't want him to think that he'd rather watch all the sexy things than do them with Pierce.

"So what will it be? *Charmed* or *Buffy*?" Rafe asked as he lay back on his pillow, inviting Pierce next to him with a pat on the mattress.

Pierce took his jacket and shoes off and warmed up next to him. "Um, *Charmed*. Of course," he answered nasally.

"See? I knew you're my kind of man," Rafe nodded and hoped Pierce got the hint.

He put an episode of the first season on and let the silence and proximity work its magic, not only on the show, but in real life too.

Halfway through, when the Halliwell sisters were facing another demon, Rafe laced his fingers with Pierce's and squeezed. When he thought he'd warmed the field enough, he turned to plant a kiss on Pierce's lips and initiate whatever needed initiating.

But Pierce was asleep.

Had he misread Pierce? Or did he bore him so much? He really thought Pierce felt the same, but apparently not. Or maybe it was his sickness that had distanced Pierce from any loving thoughts for Rafe. It was true that Pierce hadn't flirted with him since he'd told him about his positive status. Sure, he had helped him, but he had stopped being playful with Rafe. He wasn't like he was with Vance, for example. Maybe Pierce was into his boss and not Rafe. Maybe he saw Rafe like a little brother.

Rafe sighed and decided to let it go. It didn't matter. Pierce was a friend before anything, and he still wanted to show his gratitude to him. He pulled the comforter over both of them and pecked a kiss on Pierce's cheek before he resumed binge watching his favorite childhood show.

Chapter 19
Pierce

By the next week, Pierce had stayed at Rafe's every day, watching movies and TV shows, mainly from the 90s, which they both had a fascination for, going to work together, and leaving together. The upcoming Christmas craze had enveloped the city into endless green flora and Santas ringing bells on every corner. Les Fourches was bursting with tourists and families, busier than ever. Even Rafe was working a few extra shifts. Starting from this week and until the end of the season, he'd be working four shifts a week, much like Pierce. In light of the overall generosity that people subscribed to during the holiday, Pierce was counting on the Christmas spirit to put a few extra bucks in his savings.

So on Wednesday, almost a week before Christmas day, Pierce walked in for his evening shift just as Rafe was finishing his afternoon one. When he took his place behind the bar, Rafe was counting his money at the side, next to another waiter—Charlie, a hunky Australian who was doing a tour of America for a year before going off to travel the rest of the world. His trip, not so surprisingly, included humping every walking, three-legged thing. It only took a few giggles and a couple of nudges to make Pierce's insides twirl.

"Hey, Rafe. Didn't hear you leave this morning," Pierce said, approaching his friend and his colleague, adding an extra flare to his words for Charlie's enjoyment.

Rafe barely gave him a glance as he was counting. "Yeah, sorry. Didn't want to wake you," he murmured.

Pierce took the punch of Rafe's cold shoulder and tried not to look the wounded puppy he felt like. Ever since his first night at Rafe's place, there was a distance between them. Rafe no longer teased him or made double entendres about the nature of their relationship. He didn't know what he had done to distance Rafe, but he wished he could fix it. Everything he had done, and even everything he was doing now, he was doing for Rafe, to give Rafe a worthy friend. If Rafe was no longer interested in pursuing more than a work relationship with Pierce, he didn't know if he cared what happened to him. He didn't even care if he stayed on the streets 'til the end of time.

"What are you doing later, mate? Want to get a drink?" Charlie asked, elbowing Rafe's side once again.

Pierce wished he could elbow the guy's face. He hated seeing someone else touching Rafe. When Rafe smiled and gave an affirmative reply, Pierce had to shake his head and ground himself back in reality, if only to remind himself that he was just Rafe's friend and that the help he'd given came with no strings.

"Whatever time you finish, call me to open the door, okay?" Rafe told him as he put away the money and receded into the back room to hand in his cash float and his earnings.

A couple of men dressed in tight tank tops and leather shorts walked in, followed by a drag queen with fuchsia hair that towered over her head in a lopsided pyramid. All three had pink glitter eyeshadow covering their eyes and ruby red lipstick across their lips.

They all cheered when they saw Charlie, and they embraced one another in an orderly fashion. They were Conclabia and her Pubescent Pubes, a comedy act from the club two stores down. Regular customers and some of the loudest patrons.

Charlie and the gang exchanged niceties, muscle compliments, and make-up adoration before Rafe appeared and embraced each and every one of them intimately, leaving one of the Pubes for last, a tall, buff blond with brown eyes and pink blusher. He squeezed Rafe's butt cheek while they were holding the hug longer than usual, Rafe barely reacting to the violation of his privacy.

It wasn't that Pierce totally ignored Rafe's last profession, but he disliked seeing him in anyone else's arms. He considered anything mildly sexual involving Rafe as a crime against his innocence. And yes, Pierce knew that the guy he thought so innocent had been a rentboy, but he didn't think he could ever see Rafe as anything but the young kid who'd ran from home for liking Britney Spears and Katy Perry.

Rafe threw himself over the bar and pinched Pierce's nipple over his shirt. "Hey, I'm talking to you." He laughed, and so did his company.

Pierce blinked and focused on Rafe's beautiful irises staring back at him. "Yes?"

"I said, I'll see you later, *distraído*." Rafe

giggled and joined his friends in leaving the bar to start their night out somewhere farther down in the heart of the Village.

Business picked up and Pierce was forced to put Rafe—and whatever he was up to—on the backseat of his mind. The young man, however, seemed to have called shotgun on his every thought.

"Fucking dickhead," he spat while he was making a Cosmopolitan.

His colleague, also working behind the bar, turned and asked him what had happened.

"Nothing. Just…cocktails. Hate those fuckers," he murmured.

It wasn't cocktails he was pissed at, but Rafe. Why had he led him on, even going as far to invite him over to his place for a fortnight, only to blank him and date other guys? It wasn't that Pierce wanted to date Rafe, but—

No, he *did* want Rafe to be his and only his. He wanted to look at his handsome eyes all day long and hold him in his arms when he slept. He wanted to kiss those full lips and taste them for all eternity. And he wanted his touch to explore every inch of his body until he knew it by heart, but even then he wouldn't let him go because nothing was good enough as the real Rafe. Crap. He was in love with that little thieving rugrat.

Only this time, he'd stolen something

more valuable than his grandad's suitcase. He'd stolen Pierce's heart.

But what was the point, if Rafe didn't feel the same way? Since he had started on his drugs, he had proven as much; Pierce was nothing but a guest to Rafe. Gone were the hints and the hand holding that had taken place on Pierce's first night at Rafe's room, when Rafe thought he was asleep. He had felt Rafe's kiss on his cheek and he thought the next morning would be a magical one. He thought he'd wake up with Rafe by his side, kiss him good morning and stay in bed, snoozing together. But no. When he had woken up, the old Rafe was gone, leaving him with a distant one.

Before he even realized, Pierce had finished with work and had started his walk to the subway, only his destination was unknown. He didn't know what the point was to sleeping in Rafe's room when he was invisible to him. He probably wouldn't even notice if he didn't go home tonight. Hell, he probably wouldn't even be home at this time.

He made up his mind long after his legs had. And they carried him to his usual hostel. Thunder roared as he was buzzed in, and he looked at the sky before making his way to reception. The weather seemed to match his mood this evening.

"Hi, can I have a room for two nights?" Pierce asked a brunet muscular guy who was browsing Facebook on his phone.

The guy greeted him, recognizing him from other nights he'd slept over, but they had hardly ever talked.

"Sorry, dude. It seems we're all booked out for the next three weeks. Christmas time and all," he said.

Pierce frowned. "What? Where am I going to stay now?" he shouted. This just wasn't his night.

The guy shrugged and pursed his lips. "You can try the other hostels in the area," he told him.

Pierce wanted to punch the guy. He wanted to punch the wall. Instead, he slapped his hand on the desk as he was getting up. "Fine," he grunted.

He'd be damned if they saw him again. He was sure there were other hostels, much friendlier and more helpful than that douche. He stormed out just as the night storm picked up, drenching him in seconds. He made his way up a block and across the street, where he'd seen another hostel but had never slept in it. He had no luck there either. He tried another one in Uptown. He walked so far in the rain that his skin sweated while his clothes were soaking. The night was not being nice to him. He needed a place.

When he reached that hostel and they give him a negative response, he collapsed on the floor. His eyes stung like needles were poking them, and soon he was pouring his tears out, unable to control himself.

He was such a hopeless case. No one cared about him. Not his parents, certainly not Rafe. He had nothing to live for and nothing to look forward to. How had he, a college student with aspirations in life, ended up homeless and dreamless in New York?

When the sky decided to finally stop spitting its mockery on Pierce, he decided to find solace where he had a million times before. In the subway. He paid for a single ticket and let himself through the metal bars. It was way too damp at the station, so he waited for the train. He slept in intervals, changing trains and directions until the next morning when he decided to make his way to work.

To his surprise, he made it to work with barely time to spare. His phone had run out of battery, and only when he walked into the restaurant did he realize it was only ten to two. He retreated to the staff room to put on a fresh shirt and pair of jeans, fixed his greasy hair in the mirror and stepped into the bar, ready to start another shift.

Vance came from the back side carrying something. He stepped behind the bar with a case of bottled soda to restock the shelves.

"What's that smell?" he said as he passed behind Pierce.

Pierce looked around and saw his disheveled face in the mirror. "That's probably me. Sorry," he apologized.

Vance let the case on the bar and stared at Pierce, wincing. "*Why* do you smell?"

"I didn't find a hostel last night and the storm caught me," he grimaced. He didn't realize it was that bad.

Vance breathed out. "Come on, dude. One thing I told you when you started was to come to work clean."

Pierce looked at Rafe who was now sitting at the bar, having sneaked up on Pierce, who was too concerned with his boss's reprimand. "Hey, where the hell did you go last night? Why didn't you come home? I was calling you, but you weren't answering. I was so worried."

"I thought you were too busy going out with your new friends," he replied to Rafe, then turned to Vance. Why were they attacking him? Had it not been enough that he'd had a horrible night? Did they need to make him feel even crappier than he felt? "And I'm sorry I couldn't find a hostel in the middle of a high season.

Jesus!"

Vance put his hands on his waist and frowned. "Hey, Pierce, no need to give me attitude. You don't just have a case of smelly pits, you reek. If anyone should be giving anyone attitude, that's me," he said in a calm manner, but Pierce could see his nostrils flaring up as he spoke.

"Whatever," Pierce said and picked up a ticket from the printer to start making the drinks.

Vance took it from his hands. "Don't whatever me. I can't let you work in this state. Go home, dude. Have a shower and come back tomorrow," he said in the same tone.

Pierce couldn't believe his ears. What the hell was wrong with people? He thought Christmas was the time of charity, not of reckless douchebaggery. "What? I can't lose a day's worth of wages and tips," he yelled.

Vance looked at the few patrons that had turned their heads looking at the spectacle behind the bar. "Don't raise your voice with me. I said go home. I might as well work the whole day than have the whole restaurant smell like garbage," he replied with less patience.

Pierce pushed Vance. "Fuck you," he told him and turned around, leaving the bar.

"You know what? Don't bother coming back, asshole," Vance yelled having completely lost his temper.

Pierce turned and gave him the finger.

"Vance, it's okay. I can do Pierce's shift. Please, just calm down. Both of you," Rafe said, turning his head to both of them, pleading.

Pierce growled. "Of course. Swoop in and steal my job too," he shouted at Rafe.

"That's not what this is," Rafe begged and got off his chair, pulling Pierce to the staff room.

When they got in he pushed him through the door and closed it behind them.

"Have you completely lost your mind? Calm down, Pierce," he shouted as low as possible, trying not be heard outside of the room.

He took his keys out of his pocket and forced them into Pierce's hands.

"Here, take my keys and go back to my place. Have a shower. And I swear to God, if you're not there when I get back I'll whoop your fucking ass for locking me out of my apartment, and I'll whoop your fucking ass anyway for acting like an idiot," he finished and walked out of the staff room.

Pierce took his suitcase and stuffed a change of clothes from the locker inside it, then left the restaurant through the back door. He didn't want to look at anyone. He just wanted to walk. And shower. Yes, some steaming hot water didn't sound half bad at that moment.

Chapter 20
Pierce

Pierce was watching an action film when Rafe knocked on the door. He had showered, changed, and most importantly, calmed down. He was feeling like crap for what he'd done and how he'd talked to Vance, but there was nothing he could do. He had lost his job, and all he could do to sedate his anger was watch a hardcore action film.

Rafe walked in like a zombie ready to attack, his eyes half closed, his shoulders hunched forward and his hands falling lifelessly in front of him. He waved a 'Hi' and made his way to his room, where he collapsed like a big fat carcass, finding shelter under his comforter.

"How was work?" Pierce laughed.

"Busy. Very," he mumbled.

Pierce got to his knees and put his hands flat on the mattress seeking Rafe's gaze. "Listen, Rafe. I'm sorry for what I said earlier. I didn't mean any of it."

Rafe shuffled under the covers. "Oh shut up. I know. Here," he said and handed Pierce a pack of notes.

Pierce took it and stared at Rafe who had closed his eyes, resting his head on the pillow. "What's all this?"

"Your tips," came the response from the sleepy Rafe.

"My tips from where?"

"From the pits of hell. Devil says hi," Rafe muttered, still not opening his eyes. "Where do you think? The restaurant."

Pierce counted the money. There was over four hundred and fifty dollars. "What the fuck did you do? Strip in front of everyone?"

Rafe grinned. "No. Close. I smiled," he said and stretched his body, letting out a yawn.

Pierce let the comment go, something Vance and other colleagues had mentioned about him and his lack of a smile, and focused on the matter at hand. "And why are you giving it to me?"

Rafe huffed and sat up on the bed. He slapped Pierce gently on both cheeks. "Earth to Pierce. Earth to Pierce. I worked your shift, this is your money."

"No." Pierce shook his head. "That's *your* money. You worked hard for it. I can't take it," he replied.

Had Rafe lost his mind? Why was he giving him so much money when he could use it to pay more than half his rent with just a day's worth of work?

"Because I want you to get back on your feet and help you like you did with me," he rolled his eyes.

Pierce opened his mouth, staring at the man across from him. He couldn't believe what he was saying. No one in the history of ever would ever do what Rafe was doing right now, yet he was being as nonchalant about it as Pierce had been when he had chipped in from his savings to pay for Rafe's deposit and agency fees. And to think he had snapped at him that very morning. Pierce thanked him. He wished he could show him how grateful he was, but he knew Rafe probably wouldn't like it.

"You're most welcome. You just have to promise me one thing. You have to come tomorrow and apologize to Vance," he said, and his face changed to that of a teacher's telling off a student.

"What's the point?" Pierce huffed. "He fired me anyway."

Rafe slapped the side of Pierce's head. "Are you stupid? You both said words while you were angry. You can't tell me you believe that the man you went shopping with would fire you that simply."

"But—" Pierce started to say but was interrupted.

"But my butt. You will go and apologize, or I'll drag your sorry ass across town," Rafe said, stifling a weird sensation in Pierce's pants. He'd never seen Rafe so authoritative. He liked it.

The conversation had pretty much come to an end, and Rafe didn't take more than a couple of seconds to fall asleep in a fetal position. Pierce, not wanting to disrupt his sleep, took a blanket and slept on the couch in the living room. The next morning he'd already made his way to Les Fourches before it had even opened. During the festive season, they opened at nine for breakfast. At eight thirty, he knocked on the glass door and Vance let him in, looking brusquer than ever.

Pierce walked in and stood like a wet kitten in front of the man holding his fate in his hands, his chin touching his chest. "Good morning, boss," he mumbled.

"Morning," he replied with a heavy breath. "Listen, Pierce—"

"Before you say anything, I wanted to say how sorry I am. I don't know what came over me." Pierce raised his eyes to meet Vance's. "I shouldn't have talked to you like that. I know you probably don't want me back after what happened, but I wanted to apologize, nonetheless."

Pierce stood still as Vance took deep breaths without talking. His boss almost gave him a heart attack when he grasped both of his arms and searched for Pierce's face.

"You're a stupid man, Pierce, you know that? I can only imagine what your life is like, and yet I come in and basically tell you to drop dead. *I* am sorry for the way I talked to you. I mean, you're not just my employee, Pierce; you're my friend. I should have been more understanding. I am *so* sorry," he said.

Pierce blinked when salty tears formed in his eyes, and Vance gave him a tight hug.

"I wish I could do more for you. I wish I could give you full-time hours and have you work for me until you figure out what you want to do with your life. But you know I can't. Even the extra hours will go when all the tourists go back to where they came from. I might even have to let some go, considering how quiet it gets in

January," Vance told him when they'd resumed their manly positions, standing across from each other.

Pierce shook his head. "You've done more than enough, Vance. Really—" he started to say.

"You didn't let me finish. So that's what I was thinking last night, and I made some calls. Turns out, one of my exes is opening a bar in Brooklyn and is in desperate need of experienced barmen. I told him you're the best I got—even though you've only worked for me for two months—and he said he wants you. No, not want. He *needs* you," Vance said, and gave Pierce a goofy smile, bouncing on his heels.

That man could be a serious antagonist one moment and a child the next. But more than that, he was like an angel sent from whatever heavens his parents believed in. He had taken a risk hiring Pierce and then Rafe, but not only had he let them in and become their friend, he was still going the extra mile to help Pierce get back on his feet.

"That's... That's amazing," Pierce said and hugged Vance again.

His boss frowned and sucked his lips in. "The problem is it opens next week, on Christmas Eve—terrible choice. I told him so myself. But he's got like a little Christmas-slash-opening *partay*. And the thing is, I already covered all your shifts for this week. I'm sorry," Vance said and winced, waiting for Pierce to snap.

Pierce laughed. "Wait," he told him, "you've found me a full-time job, and you're afraid I will snap at you? Right now you're my favorite human being on this entire world."

"I bet after Rafe," Vance chuckled and went in for a pinch at Pierce's stomach, which Pierce slapped away, grinning like an idiot.

Pierce stayed for breakfast at the restaurant, and when Rafe got in for his afternoon shift, he asked for the keys and made his way back to the flat. He didn't know how to spend his time not working, so he decided to grab another book from a used bookstore, having finished the one he'd been reading for over a month now. The one book turned to two, and when the time came the week after to start his first shift at his new job, he had collected almost an entire collection of copies, all resting on top of Rafe's sketchbooks.

Rafe had been overjoyed that Pierce had got a new job but was sad that they wouldn't work together anymore.

"At least we'll be seeing each other every night," he'd told him, only to be reminded by Pierce that their elongated slumber party would only last another week, when Rafe's landlord would return from his holidays and Pierce would have to find another hostel, one that wasn't completely booked out.

"I got used to having you around. I'll miss our movie nights," Rafe said.

Pierce grimaced, feeling as nostalgic as Rafe, as if their fun together had ceased already, and as if they'd been doing movie nights for years.

"We can still have movie nights. Just not *every day* like we're doing now," he said, trying to lighten the mood.

Before the twenty-sixth came to bite him in the ass — the day when Wang returned from his vacation — Pierce booked a hostel for a whole month so that he wouldn't run the risk of staying homeless again. When the twenty-fourth came and he was going to start his new job, he was all set to start the new chapter in his life.

The bar in Brooklyn was called O'Neill's Debauchery, and as its logo it had a cartoon shamrock holding a glass of Guinness, puking little shamrocks. As goofy as their sign was, it was nothing compared to the inside and the boss.

On a first glance, Pierce would never guess his new boss, Sam, was gay, especially an ex to the charming and lively Vance. Sam was chubby, dark-haired, with a messy beard and glasses. He was wearing a Marvel T-shirt and had tribal tattoos down his arms. He was, however, very effeminate in his speech and his mannerisms..

He seemed excited to have Pierce on his team, and they had a good hour's chat over beer before he gave him a small tour of the place.

Sam explained that he only needed two full-timers, with some part-timers for the weekends, but that after January it would probably be only Pierce, another girl, and himself left to run the place. Pierce started his shift at four, showing Sam all the cocktails he knew how to make and experimenting with some new flavors, because Sam had still not decided what special drinks to put on the menu. He wanted all the drinks to have an Irish touch and kept asking for Pierce's opinion. It was too bad that Pierce was really not in touch with his Irish side, other than his suitcase which belonged to his Irish immigrant of a grandfather. Sam didn't have any of the heritage, he just loved St. Patrick's Day and wanted to put a shot of Guinness in all the cocktails, something Pierce had to convince him not to do.

The party started at six. People filed in, filling up the entire bar—which was half the size of Les Fourches—until Pierce and his colleague, a trans girl called Rosie, were working non-stop, serving complimentary drinks to all the guests and pocketing a dollar for every serving.

Then around nine, Sam gave a small speech, and Pierce and Rosie helped themselves to a glass of champagne with their boss.

Rosie was twenty-five and lived in the area. She was Sam's current girlfriend and was also a postgraduate student in business management. She and Sam had been together for almost two years when she had first started transitioning. She was a sweet girl with a lot of experience in bartending. When Pierce asked her what she wanted to do when she finished, she told him she wanted to run the business with Sam, which Pierce hadn't expected. He was used to being surrounded by artists of all walks of life and in various stages in their career but had not met one that wanted to be a bartender for the rest of their life. Pierce couldn't even grasp the concept of working behind a bar for another year, let alone a lifetime. Not that he had any clue what he wanted to do. He just knew the bar was only temporary. Hopefully.

At two, O'Neill's Debauchery closed, and after cleaning and tidying up the place for Boxing Day, since the bar would remain closed on Christmas Day, Pierce phoned Rafe to tell him how great his first shift had gone. He turned left on the street, only two blocks away from the apartment, when two guys started following him. They were both smoking marijuana and shadowing his every move.

"Um, I think I'm being followed," Pierce

whispered on the line while stealing glances behind him, pretending to be checking the traffic.

"What?" Rafe shrieked over the phone. "Find a busy street and lights, Pierce. Run. I don't know. Where are you?"

He was left with no time to respond; the phone was punched out of his hand.

"Hey, dickface, where you goin'?" one of the guys slurred behind him.

Pierce avoided looking at either one of them and bent down to pick up his phone. He regretted it immediately.

A firm foot came crashing up his stomach. He tried to find his balance, but he was pushed to the ground.

"Whatchu got in the bag? Huh?" the other guy said and tried to snatch Pierce's suitcase from his hands.

"Nothing. Clothes," Pierce stuttered. "Just clothes."

Rafe shouted something on the phone, but Pierce was too focused on not letting go of his suitcase to care. The guy was pulling hard, but Pierce didn't cave in. That bag had all his savings in it. Rafe had suggested he keep them at his house, but being stubborn as he was, he hadn't listened, a choice he regretted now. He made a mental note to listen to Rafe next time. If there was a next time.

"Mother—" The guy wouldn't let go of his suitcase either and resorted to dragging Pierce onto the sidewalk, trying to snatch it away from him.

While Pierce was grinding with the ground, he managed to give himself a boost and stand up. Another choice he regretted. The other guy, who was now trying to pull Pierce on the other side and away from his possession, put his hand under his coat and pulled out something silvery.

His insides screamed with pain, and bile traveled up his throat as he got sick on the sidewalk. The guy had slashed a knife into his stomach. A quick glance at his shirt told him the blood was pouring out as fast as he felt his veins pumping.

His hands loosened and the guy finally took hold of the suitcase. He knelt down and opened it up.

"Dude, this dude is a goldmine. Look at that," he said, flashing his accomplice the pack of Pierce's money.

Pierce made a last attempt to claim his suitcase back. They could have the money if they wanted, but he'd die before he let them take the suitcase. He grabbed the edge of it.

When he did, two things happened. First, the street was washed with blue and red lights before the siren even pierced everyone's ears. Second, the thugs made a run for it, pulling the suitcase open, all its contents falling onto the ground, and dragging Pierce a few more feet ahead. Seeing Pierce's resistance, they gave up on the suitcase. Pierce heard the commotion, but everything started to go out. First the streetlights. Then the sirens. And last, all voices. Even his voice, begging whoever was coming to his rescue to save his suitcase.

Chapter 21
Rafe

e opened his eyes just as the nurse was leaving the room. Rafe had been by Pierce's side in the hospital, only leaving it to grab a quick bite and to use the bathroom. It hurt him too much to see Pierce bandaged and tubed up. He couldn't possibly step into work and do a good job. Vance had given him as many days off as he needed to look after Pierce, and that was exactly what he was going to do.

"Hey, *bruto*, good morning," Rafe greeted him with a warm smile.

Pierce looked disoriented, eyes not yet focused. When they did, though, they fell on

Rafe.

"Where am I?" His voice was hoarse and no more distinguishable than a growl.

"In Heaven. And I'm St. Peter," Rafe answered, getting up from his chair and taking Pierce's head in his hands as though he was going to bless him. "Where do you think you are? The hospital, silly."

Pierce jumped up, but folded in pain as soon as he did, withering on the bed.

"Take it slow, *chulo*. You're still not healed, you know. Do you want to pop a stitch or something?" Rafe scolded him and fixed the pillow to help Pierce set back on it.

"How—" Pierced started but had to take frequent breaths in order to be audible. "How long have I been here?"

Rafe covered him with the blanket and flattened it on him. "Two days," he told him.

Pierce sat up in protest, but Rafe pushed him back down, knowing he would panic.

"But…I can't afford this, Rafe. I got to go," he insisted, trying to ward his hands off, but Rafe held firm.

Rafe winced and put his hand on Pierce's heart. "*You* almost fucking *died*. You need to heal, so you're going to stay as long as it's needed to do just that, or I swear to God, I'll kill you myself."

Rafe wasn't angry with Pierce. He was angry with what the thugs had done to him. And he was frustrated that Pierce could be thinking about money over his health.

When the police officer had picked up Pierce's cell on the street and told him that his friend had passed out, Rafe nearly did the same. When they told him where to go, he got the first cab and rushed to Pierce's side. He *had* almost died, but the good doctors of St. Andrew had saved him. He'd be damned if he let Pierce kill himself with his stubbornness after all Rafe had been through.

Pierce's head dropped onto his chest and he sucked his lips, apologizing to Rafe.

Rafe threw him a threatening look to ensure his message still held true, and Pierce let out a chuckle that made him cough. Rafe gave him some water.

"What happened to me?" he asked when he'd calmed down.

Rafe sat back down and told him all he had suffered through. "The knife cut through your stomach and some veins. You were hemorrhaging on the scene, and when the ambulance arrived, you had lost a lot of blood. They had to transfuse you with a ton of it. Then, you went through sepsis because of a bacterial infection. That was when I…we nearly lost you. But you made it through.

Then of course you had a high fever for so many hours that you had to be in the ER for constant supervision. The fever, thankfully, subsided, and they brought you out last night. You've been sleeping ever since," Rafe explained, realizing when he'd finished that his words had turned to sobs that he had to push through to be heard.

Pierce looked outside. "Fuck!" was all he said, and Rafe wiped his eyes quickly before Pierce turned back at him. "And you stayed here all this time? Didn't you miss work?"

Rafe cursed at him. He couldn't believe he was *still* thinking about work. This guy! He was all about the money. That's what got him into trouble in the first place. If he hadn't accepted Vance's invitation to work in the Brooklyn bar, none of this would have happened.

"Thank you," Pierce murmured, barely heard in Rafe's deafening mind. He looked up to see Pierce with red eyes. "For—for being here… for me," he said.

Rafe got up and approached the bed to give him a hug. "You, idiot. When will you realize I'd do anything for you?"

Pierce chuckled into Rafe's chest, still embracing him. Rafe closed his eyes. He liked this: the warmth of Pierce's body on his, the strength of his hands around him, sizzling the skin and everything under it, wherever they touched him. The feeling of Pierce's breath tickled his ribs. He could stay there forever if Pierce let him.

But Pierce pushed him away and jerked his head around. "Where—where is my suitcase?"

Rafe knew they'd get to that eventually. He didn't know how to bring the news to him, so with a bit of hesitation, he pulled the suitcase out from behind the bedside table. "Um, all the money is gone, Pierce. And uh—" he paused and presented the broken down suitcase.

Pierce put it on his lap and opened it. The top part fell off. The pictures were still inside, although some were muddied up and ripped at the edges.

"They said you tried to hold on to it. And it broke apart. I'm sure you can fix it somewhere, though. It's just the pictures. Some of them are really bad. All there—I checked—but…" Rafe trailed off, not knowing how else to explain what had happened to Pierce's and his grandad's memories.

Pierce could see it for himself. One picture was faded to the point that he had to squint to make out anything. Some others were covered in dry mud. "How—how did this happen?"

"I don't know. I think some fell in a puddle, and the guys who actually picked them up didn't bother drying them, so they kinda faded. I don't know; I wasn't there." Rafe grimaced, looking at Pierce going through all the pictures. "I wish I was."

Pierce put them down, back inside the suitcase, and took Rafe's hands. "I don't. They might have hurt you too if you had been there. And *I* don't know if I could live with that."

Someone knocked on the door before Rafe could answer, and the nurse waltzed back in. "Oh, you're up. Awesome. How are you feeling, Pierce?" she asked with a gentle smile stamped on her face.

"Like a truck ran over me," Pierce answered, and the nurse laughed.

"Well, not really. But close," she giggled. "I'm sorry to bother you—I know you've just woken up—but we need your insurance details. Your friend here didn't know them. We tried contacting your parents as well. We called the number on our records, but the person who replied said they didn't know a Pierce Callahan. Is it possible that it's a wrong number?"

"It's the right number." Pierce mumbled.

Rafe saw Pierce react to what the nurse had told him, and he looked as if he'd been stabbed a second time. Fucking parents. They were both better without them. Rafe squeezed Pierce's hand, and he found the strength to tell the nurse he didn't have insurance. They spent the next hour discussing the details of potential insurances and discharging him, something that Rafe objected to, but ultimately it wasn't up to him. Since Pierce was uninsured, every hour he spent in the hospital was accumulating, and since he was broke, they needed him out as soon as he could stand on his feet.

Rafe called a cab and took him back to his place. Thankfully, Wang had extended his vacation unexpectedly, so Pierce had a place to stay until then, although he'd refuse to kick his friend in the curb even if his landlord didn't like it. Wang was a nice man; he was sure he'd understand and have no problem with Pierce staying until he could recover.

As soon as Pierce had gone back to sleep, Rafe called Vance to let him know about Pierce's progress and to discuss the week's shifts. Vance sounded relieved that Pierce was better. When he hung up, Rafe skimmed through Wang's bookcase and found a recipe book. He made a list of the ingredients he needed for a pho soup and popped to the nearest store to pick them up.

When Pierce woke up, he was surprised with a nice Vietnamese dinner.

"Just don't make it a habit, okay?" Pierce commented and slurped another spoonful of soup.

"Why?" Rafe asked.

"Because you're spoiling me, and you're wasting your money," he said.

Rafe rolled his eyes and slapped Pierce in the head. It seemed as if it was going to be his signature move with this guy, slapping him. Maybe he'd slap some sense into him eventually.

Chapter 22
Pierce

Pierce came out of the shower groaning and grabbing his stomach where a plastic film covered his bandages and kept his stitches dry. It was New Year's Eve and Rafe was working the afternoon shift, surprisingly so. Since Pierce had left Les Fourches, Rafe had gone on to doing both waiting and bartending shifts, working full-time, even after the end of the festive season. One of the waiters had quit, and Vance had decided to keep Rafe as a permanent employee since he had proven himself an amazing worker. Pierce was proud of him.

When he'd changed clothes and bandages,

he lay back down on the bed and took Wang's laptop on his lap to resume his watching of Star Trek. That Zachary Quinto was so freaking hot, even with the pointy ears and the appalling haircut. Not that he would tell Rafe that, though. He took the chips from the shelf above the bed and snacked on them. At least the intense pain had stopped and he could actually enjoy something other than sleep. The painkillers helped. And Quinto did too, which was why he was watching the same film for the fifth time in a row. Chris Pine wasn't bad either.

He heard the door open and paused the film. He wasn't sure when Wang was supposed to be back, today or tomorrow, but he didn't want him to know he had possession of his laptop when he'd only seen the guy once. Rafe hadn't even had the chance to tell him Pierce was staying over while he was recovering. He grabbed his stomach and stood, swallowing the groan, and started to open the door. It swung open and Rafe walked in, making Pierce lose his footing and fall back on the mattress.

"Shit. Are you okay?" Rafe dropped to the floor, checking on Pierce.

Pierce grimaced. "You scared the crap out of me," he spat, and Rafe laughed.

"Whatchu doing?" Rafe asked and his eyes fell on the laptop screen. "Swooning over

Captain Kirk and Spock again? I told you, find someone more feasible to obsess over. They're a lost case. Plus, I think they're screwing each other," Rafe said and put down a massive red glittery bag.

Pierce grinned. He had found someone more realistic to obsess over, but he couldn't possibly tell him that. Ever since he had woken up in the hospital with Rafe by his side, he thought that perhaps he had misjudged Rafe's interest in him. Sure, they were friends, but he felt Rafe was closer than a friend. He felt as if Rafe was his boyfriend. He certainly treated him as such. Rafe cooked for him and picked new books up for him and stroked his hair at night when Pierce was in pain and trying to sleep through it.

"What've you got in the bag?" he asked.

Rafe pushed it farther away from Pierce when he started to see what was inside. "First things first. I've brought food. Italian. I was gonna go for Mexican, but with your fucked up stomach, I didn't know how spicy you can handle," he told him.

Pierce laughed. "I can't handle spicy on a good stomach, so—"

Rafe gasped and shook his head, rolling his eyes. "I can't believe my…friend doesn't eat spicy. Jeez-us!"

Pierce chuckled and apologized.

"I'm kidding. I can't handle very spicy food, either. Anyway, I've got vegan tortellini with basil and tomato filling for the both of us and a green salad to share. Also dropped by that vegan bakery on 18th and bought some vanilla cheesecake made from cashew and coconut. I'll admit, I tried a bit on the way here. It was ah-mazing," Rafe said, then disappeared in the kitchen.

Pierce smiled. Further proof that Rafe was his boyfriend without either of them knowing it. He had changed to a vegan diet without Pierce ever asking him to. He just had. Obviously working in a vegetarian restaurant helped the palate, but Pierce was astounded with how far this young, sick rentboy had come. Working a full-time job, fully medicated and healthy, changing diet for the sake of his…friend. How could Pierce possibly tell Rafe that he didn't think they were friends without risking their relationship? Pierce might think they were more like boyfriends, but perhaps that was how Rafe was with all his friends. He was certainly close with all the gays that frequented Les Fourches.

He returned with plates and cranberry juice in wine glasses. "I thought since you can't drink alcohol and I can't buy it, we'd fake it," Rafe explained and passed a glass to Pierce.

The clinked their glasses and commenced

their feasting. Everything was delicious. Everything tasted better with Rafe by his side, laughing and smiling. Pierce was happy, even in his misery. When they'd finished their dessert, Rafe took the plates back to the kitchen and came back, closing the door behind him. He made the short way across the room and picked up the red bag.

"And now for the surprise," he said and gave the bag to Pierce.

Pierce took it but kept his gaze on Rafe. "What's this?"

"It's my Christmas present for you. It was a bit delayed, what with missing work and you nearly dying, but it still counts, right?" Rafe shrugged and held his shoulder next to his face, waiting for Pierce's reply.

Pierce was lost for words. He opened it and retrieved a square box wrapped in blue paper with snowmen in different sexual positions. He laughed, tearing through it. The box was revealed to be camera. A DSLR. He winced and shook the box, then opened the flap to find that it did actually contain a digital camera.

"What—is—this?" he asked, still not believing that this was his present.

Rafe sat on the bed next to him. "It's used. I'm sorry; I wanted to buy a new one, but those fuckers are really expensive," he commented.

Pierce shook his head. "Yeah, but—why? Why did you spend so much money on a gift like that?" Pierce took the little machine out of its nest and explored every single of its inches.

"I work full time now; I don't have to pay for my meds, plus I worked some extra shifts at the restaurant. I mean, I had to go out with fucking Conclabia and her Pubes to get the regulars to tip more…and it worked," Pierce was looking at Rafe in disbelief.

Was that why he had withdrawn from Pierce and was hanging out with colleagues and patrons more?

"I wanted you to have your own memories and stop living through your grandad's. That's why I got this camera for you. So that you take your own pictures and believe in a better future. I know you can't travel…yet, but I hoped—" Rafe continued and his eyes were red and he was smiling and he was looking into Pierce's eyes and Pierce into his.

Pierce didn't let him finish. He leaned closer and pressed his lips to Rafe's. They were moist and full and so warm. Everything felt right at that moment. He put his hand in Rafe's hair, and it felt like coming home. Rafe placed his hand on Pierce's chest, and it felt like that was where they should have been all along. And Rafe was kissing him back with so much tenderness.

With a little bit of hesitation, Pierce asked for permission with his tongue to be let into Rafe's mouth and he let him, and before he knew it they were both lying on the bed, clasping each other's hands tight. Rafe rubbed his body against Pierce's. Pierce's body awakened in Rafe's arms. He had been waiting a long time for this. A groan escaped his lips, and they both trembled with the vibration, their lips still locked together, as if they'd been glued and could never be separated.

"About damn time, my sweet bruto," Rafe mumbled.

Pierce moaned again. "I thought you didn't like me," he muttered.

He wished he hadn't, because Rafe pulled back. "Are you actually stupid or pretending to be? I was literally begging you to kiss me since the day I robbed you."

"Why didn't you say anything?"

Rafe sat up. "Because I thought my body was screaming it," he waved his hands around and laughed. He dropped back into Pierce's arms. "I'm sorry," he said. "I'm not good with flirting."

"Yeah, no kidding," Rafe responded.

"Well, it's not like I got as much experience as you do," Pierce said.

Rafe sat up again. "Yeah, 'cause it takes a love-veteran to hook up. How did you get with other guys?"

Pierce bit his lip. "I've never...actually been with anyone."

Rafe widened his eyes and pursed his lips in a sad face. Pierce pushed him back.

"No need to pity me, idiot," he said.

Rafe laughed. "Surely you've kissed others. Your lips say so."

Pierce nodded. "Of course I have. Now will you let me shut your mouth with my experienced lips?" He pulled Rafe back down on him. Rafe's weight fell on the left side of Pierce's body, where his wound was, and he growled. Rafe jumped back up.

"I'm okay. Don't...don't ever leave my side again," Pierce said and tugged Rafe back on him, more gently this time, and kissed his lips. It already felt like centuries since the last time he'd touched them. And it would probably be an eternity before he let him go again.

"Happy New Year, bruto," Rafe muttered between breaths.

"Happy New Year, baby," Pierce replied. They both smiled. It was going to be a good year. They were together now.

Chapter 23
Pierce

The next morning when Rafe's alarm went off, piercing through the buzzing silence of the room, they woke up in each other's arms. Rafe was the first to move toward his phone and turn the annoying sound off before Pierce opened his eyes and stretched his upper body. He remembered too late that he shouldn't be doing that and folded in two.

"I keep forgetting I've got that fucking thing on my stomach," he mumbled under the sheets.

"You better get used to it, 'cause the last thing we want is to break the stitches now that they're starting to heal," Rafe retorted.

Pierce recovered from the pain and looked at Rafe. "Good morning," he smiled.

"Good morning," Rafe said and leaned in to kiss him.

"Why are you up so early?" Pierce asked, pulling the blanket back up to his neck.

Rafe put his forehead to Pierce's and wiggled his nose. He planted a kiss on Pierce's nose before answering. "I'm working a double today. So I won't be home until at least midnight."

Pierce opened his eyes and looked at Rafe, who was taking off the T-shirt he had slept in, the same he had worked in the previous day, and pulling out another one from his propped-up wardrobe. He didn't want to let him go. He wanted to pull him back in bed and explore what he hadn't had the chance to yet.

"Be careful on your way back. Take a cab. I don't want you getting robbed or hurt too," he said.

Rafe told him not to worry. He put his rucksack around his back, gave Pierce a big kiss, and left the house. Which left Pierce all on his own. With a new camera to explore. At least he wouldn't spend all day reading and watching TV again. Not that he could do the latter. He had to take the laptop and put it back in the living room before Wang returned. If he hadn't already.

He tiptoed through the hallway and peeked around when he reached the living room. Nothing had been touched. Everything was as it had been left by the landlord before he left. Pierce set the laptop down on the coffee table with its charger and retreated back into the room where he got dressed. He put his shoes on and took his new-old camera in his hands, checked that it worked and that it had an SD card, and left the apartment, excited to find out what it could do.

He played around a bit with it, getting the feel of it in his hand, getting used to its weight and its lens. It was a standard 50mm with an aperture of 4.3, but he liked the effect it had on his depth of field. He used to have cameras when he was younger, so he was familiar with their settings and use, but anything he'd owned in the past was usually put to use during family vacations and school trips. He'd tried to venture into sports photography during college, for the extra credit if not for the sweaty, steaming view of athletes at their best, but he hadn't had a chance or the wish to take it any further than that. Photography was always on the back of his mind as an interest rather than nagging at him on the forefront as a passion.

He started with objects—a tree here, a sign there, a blurred view of the city traffic, the sky, parked cars. Things he'd seen before but looked enchanting through the glass of the lens. By lunchtime, he had started taking pictures of people as they went about their business. He would snap a businessman on his way back to work from the bar, the woman carrying her shopping and panting as if she'd run a mile, the employee nursing a good, long cigarette on the back street before returning to work. Every single human being that he passed by spoke to him in a way no one had ever in the eight months he'd been living on the streets. It was as if they were no longer the heartless passersby who were unwilling to help but the gentle souls who did their best to survive the mundane life as a New Yorker.

Some hundred pictures later, he found out he couldn't take his eyes off people anymore, kept looking for things that made them stand apart from the mass. He was sure most of the photos he'd snapped were useless, and the ones that weren't were probably wrong as fuck in artistic terms, but he didn't care for the end result. Looking through the viewfinder and searching for his next victim, all he cared about was being one with them at that moment, the instant that it took to connect with them, finding the exact second to immortalize in pixels.

When his stomach curled and he felt like

it would start gushing out of his entry wound, he decided to make his way to Manhattan to get some lunch and afterward visit some of his old haunts. As intense as Brooklyn was, Manhattan was the absolute extreme, with people wearing diamonds in one street and people going through the trash in the next. He wanted to see if he could capture that dichotomy of the island. He used some of Rafe's change that he'd left behind for Pierce and bought a subway ticket, riding on the train to Times Square, where he'd start his journey—after grabbing some noodles from the closest street vendor, of course.

Half an hour later he was finishing a good cashew chow mein on top of Pavilion while tourists were going crazy, snapping photos on their iPhones, Galaxies, iPads, and anything else they'd spent a fortune on that had the exact same function. Pierce got up and disposed of his meal, wiping his hands on the trillion napkins he'd snatched from the man. The last thing he wanted was to soil his brand new toy.

He placed it back in his hands, palms finding comfort on the plastic, and ventured into the jungle that he was starting to appreciate. The streets that had been so kind, offering him shelter, the buildings that were hiding hostility and superior attitude, the businesses that had offered him judgment, the people that had turned a blind eye. But all that was in the past for him. All he felt when he thought of the last few months was the great job he'd managed to find that offered him so little but so much for a guy who had nothing. The friends he'd made. Vance, perhaps the most down-to-earth boss anyone could ever have. Damian, the Jekyll-and-Hyde business geek that still enjoyed fairy tales. Marissa, the goth girl who made the best out of her situation. Sam and Rosie, the pair that had found love in each other and their shared passion for the hospitality industry. And of course, Rafe, the kid who had tried to steal his suitcase but ended up taking something far more valuable in the end.

He wanted to show the world those opposing sides of the city that never sleeps. He wanted to tell his story through his own eyes, his own lens. Many people had tried to do what he'd done. None of them had shown the much darker side that lay on the other side of the middle-class musicals and the celebrities flashing fake smiles at the paparazzi. Or maybe there had been others. He didn't care. He didn't want to do it for anyone but him. It wasn't as if he had anyone other than Rafe to show the pictures anyway. But he wanted to make them good. Gramps Kevan had snapped his life away on his camera; it was time for Pierce to snap his.

And he did. He went by the homeless shelter that had required a blowjob on registration and took pictures of the people outside, carrying unfolded sleeping bags, walking on slippers with no socks on. He went by Central Park, where the drunk old man had managed to buy a bottle of booze and was downing it, remembering all that he had once been and all he could have been before life slapped him hard across the face. He went by the street where Rafe had sold his body and took the pictures of boys from all walks of life selling the last dignified thing they owned over and over again. He went by Mario's and snapped pictures of Sonia and her charitable smile, giving to everyone when she had so little. He went by Les Fourches and, without entering, recorded photographs of a hopeless case, rebuilding a future behind the bar.

And as he was standing across the street, looking at Rafe from inside his camera, the longing burning in his chest gave him purpose. He didn't want to work bars for the rest of his life. He knew that. And he didn't want to take pictures for the rest of his life, although it was a welcome addition to his lean hobby list. What he did want was to see that smile on Rafe's face. But he didn't want to see it only on Rafe. He wanted to see it on the drunks, the junkies, the survivalists, on all those people who been defecated on by life and were still here, still alive, still praying, and still hoping. He wanted to be that hope.

Right there, right then he decided. He'd fight until his last breath to achieve his dream. He might not have had a clue how to go about it, but he would. And with that thought, he finished his day's session and walked into the restaurant where he knew a free and delicious meal awaited him.

Chapter 24
Rafe

hen Rafe finished his shift and all his money was handed in, he sat down with Pierce, giving him a big smooch. Ever since he'd started, everyone always asked if he was hooking up with Pierce, and now that he finally had, he wanted everyone to know.

Pierce informed him that he had taken a ton of pictures and couldn't wait to show him, and he couldn't wait to see them. He couldn't wait to be alone with his boyfriend. He had been thinking of Pierce's sweet kisses all day long. How cozy it was nested in Pierce's big arms and racing heart.

"Oh, would you two get a room?" Vance exclaimed as he took a seat on their table, gagging at the look of the new couple.

Some of the waiters were waving goodbye before closing the door behind them.

"Um…" Pierce stared at his old boss and got his attention. "Fuck off, Vance. And I say that from the bottom of my heart," he said.

Vance grinned and sat back on his chair. "You guys are so cute together. What the fuck took you so long?"

Neither one of them answered that. They preferred to look into each other's eyes instead. Pierce stretched his hand on the table and Rafe laced his fingers with Pierce's.

"Do you guys want to get a drink at Marcy's before you go shack up?" Vance asked, looking at their hands instead of their faces, the creases around his eyes making it obvious his mind was now somewhere else.

Rafe looked back at Pierce and nodded knowingly. Vance wanted to talk or take his mind off something, and they'd be total pigs if they didn't help their friend. "Sure thing, Vance."

Vance shook his head as if waking from sleep and nodded in agreement. "That's fine," he said, "I've done my wild boozing last night."

Rafe downed the remainder of his beer,

for once not in a mug but in an actual pint glass, helped Pierce stand up, and helped Vance close down the bar. They walked across the street and around the block, where Marcy's was situated under flashing lights and risqué posters of drag queens and go-go dancers. One of them was of Conclabia and her Pubescent Pubes. Tonight was live rock music, so they didn't have to endure the waxing act of the sexually deprived drag queen and her sexually charged dancers.

They walked in and climbed the stairs to the mezzanine where Vance had a table reserved on a nightly basis. Their waiter, a nicely dressed young man with a terrible fringe covering half his face, took their order for a dry martini and two virgin Cosmos and left them to their peace, where Vance could finally pour his heart out about whatever was bothering him.

"So you wanna tell us what happened or wait for the drinks to get them to get you to tell us?" Pierce asked with a discernible grin. Rafe nudged his arm next to him.

Vance looked up at them and crossed his hands on his lap. "What are you talking about?"

"Come on." Rafe rolled his eyes. "Something is *clearly* bothering you, boss."

Vance winced. "*Chico*, you know me so well."

Pierce chuckled and held his stomach

to restrain himself from laughing any harder. "Dude, the fucking singer can tell you've got the blues, and he ain't even a blues singer."

"Okay, okay. You got me. I just had a stupid night yesterday so I'm just not feeling very…uppity," Vance admitted, holding his hands up in surrender.

Rafe tapped his hand on the table, demanding the beans. "Spill them," he shouted over the music.

Vance huffed and looked at the ceiling. "Well, you know the *friend* I was supposed to spend my New Year's Eve with?" They both nodded. "Well, he was sort of a date."

Pierce and Rafe turned to look at each other while Vance was being coy with them. "No joke," Pierce commented.

"Anyway," he ignored both of them and continued, "we went out last night, I put on my new suit, we went somewhere nice and expensive, and as we were talking he started mentioning his boyfriend. You know, 'my boyfriend this, my boyfriend that'…"

"I thought you said it was a date," Rafe said.

"I did too," Vance retorted. "I hadn't seen him in ages. When he got back in touch with me he was being very funny and flirty, and I genuinely thought he was interested. But he was only interested in business tips and how to get started in New York. He wants to open his own restaurant, and *apparently* I'm the only one he knows who's got a business," Vance sighed.

Pierce whistled. "What a Debby Downer. Sorry, dude, but please…"

"…don't tell me you're down because of him?" Rafe interrupted to also scold at Vance.

Vance nodded. "Well, I really liked this guy. I mean I've known him for like ten years, but I met him when I was with my then-boy-friend. By the time I became single again, he moved out to L.A. and stuff. So he contacted me, I really thought he was interested. Our message history certainly read as such. And, I don't know guys, I'm sick of all the fucking frogs I have to kiss. When is *my* prince gonna arrive? I'm not getting any younger." He pursed his lips and the waiter arrived with their drinks. Vance took hold of his before it was given to him.

Rafe and Pierce spent the rest of the night consoling their depressed boss, trying to convince him that his life hadn't ended and that he would find his soulmate, if such thing existed. At around two a.m. they decided to make their way back to the apartment and got on the subway.

"He's only thirty-six for crying out loud," Pierce exclaimed. "Gay guys are such big, fat drama queens."

Rafe laughed. "Come on, give him a break. He's been through a lot of relationships. It's natural to lose hope. Especially when guys have fucked him up so badly."

"Yeah, I know. And he's such a catch as well. I don't get it," Pierce said.

"I know. Me neither," Rafe agreed.

Pierce found Rafe's hand on the seat between them and held it. "You're not gonna fuck me up, are you?"

Rafe looked at him and put his forehead on Pierce's. Those damn eyes. Blue like the morning sky, lit with such glimmering desperation, hanging off Rafe's reply as if they depended on him to keep their spark. Rafe couldn't believe he was even asking him that.

"Never, you stupid," he told him and gave him a gentle kiss.

Pierce's cheeks puffed up and Rafe saw them blushing despite the smile.

They got off at their stop and got to the apartment in no time. Wang was still not back, so Rafe sneaked his laptop into his bedroom so Pierce could show him all the beautiful pictures he'd taken. Pierce inserted the SD card and clicked the camera folder that popped up on the screen.

The first few pictures were urban shots that he'd seen a thousand times on posters, Facebook,

TV shows, portraits. They looked like the pictures that tourists take of every single thing they see in their destination as if they'd never seen it before and never would again. There were a few that were stunning in their perception, especially for a photography fledgling like his boyfriend, but the majority were dull and uninteresting. Not that he let Pierce know that. He didn't want to burst his bubble. Besides, it wasn't as if the pictures were for display. They were for Pierce to create memories, and if those were the memories he wanted to make, who was he to stop him?

But then something magical happened.

The pictures were no longer about inanimate or animated objects but of people of every color and walk of life. He'd managed to get shots of people doing private things in the ever-so-public and always-busy streets of the Big Apple. The shot of a woman in a red suit lighting a cigarette while holding a telephone with her shoulder. A man picking oranges to put in a grocery bag. A young girl blowing a bubble. A boy's attempt at a skating trick. One by one those pictures revealed a talent he didn't know Pierce possessed. Not only had he taken nice colorful pictures, he had also taken soulful pictures.

And then they got to snapshots of a life he knew well. He saw the homeless with their carts, scavenging in trash; men, women, and children sleeping on carton boxes. He even saw the street he'd spent a year at, picking up customers for a dirty business he wished he'd never have to go back to.

"Those are so beautiful, *chulo*," he told him, snuggled up next to him in the single bed, with only the peaceful light of the fairy lights casting a warm tone to the room.

"You mean that?" Pierce asked in a hushed voice.

Rafe smiled. "Yes," he confirmed, and Pierce's shy look made him give in.

He'd been feeling it all night, since he saw him walking in Les Fourches with his sapphire coat and camera in hand, like a model posing for a magazine cover. He'd felt it whenever he held his hand and his fingers massaging the back of it. He'd felt it sitting next to him at Marcy's, consoling Vance, but doing so with such happiness he couldn't help but feel like a hypocrite during Vance's heart-to-heart. He'd felt it in the subway train, casting away Pierce's fears, and he was feeling it now, seeing the talent that oozed out of him.

He wanted this man. This *bruto* who had patched his heart back up after his parents had shattered it to pieces. This tough guy who had gone out of his way to help him get back on his feet. This vulnerable soul that needed more love than Rafe could possibly give him. He couldn't wait any longer. He wanted to be one with him.

And so he kissed him. Pierce kissed back while placing the laptop on the floor between the bed and the wall, and his hands came back more triumphant, grabbing Rafe's waist as he went in for a deeper kiss. Rafe could almost chuckle at how inexperienced this big, muscular guy was compared to him, and how badly it showed on Pierce's delicate moves, who touched Rafe as if he was afraid to break him. But instead of laughing, it turned him on. It was sexier than someone who knew his way around the game like his clients. Most of them were so seasoned in sexing-up that they'd forgotten all the good bits and skipped straight to the action. But Rafe didn't want that with Pierce. Pierce wasn't a money machine, nor a bed until the next morning. With him, Rafe wanted to explore the art of lovemaking. An art he'd only explored with one other person: the person who had cost him his good health.

He shook the image of his first boyfriend out of his mind and focused on his current one, still afraid to touch anywhere but the waist and face. Rafe took Pierce's hand and put it on his ass, placing his own on Pierce's. His hand squeezed the firm, full buttock, and his cock in his jeans ached as it grew harder. The closeness was already making him sweat, and they hadn't even started yet.

He put his hand under Pierce's jeans so that he could feel the smoothness of his buttock and pulled him closer where his cock could rub against his boyfriend's, and from the feel of it, Pierce was as painfully hard as he was. He wanted to touch it, but he was sure if he did, he would shoot a load in his jeans. So instead he turned Pierce on the mattress so that he was lying fully on his back and sat on his lap. Pierce's cock pulsed under his groin. Rafe moaned. Pierce couldn't seem to take his eyes off Rafe. He felt his stare heating up his face.

Rafe grabbed Pierce's T-shirt and took it off so that he could admire the body he'd been craving for months. He saw the bandaged wound on the left, under his ribs, and made a mental note to not go any rougher on him. He'd probably have to do all the work while Pierce lay down, but he didn't mind. He wanted to worship the body of his boyfriend like he deserved. He dived in for another kissing session, which Pierce starved for. His lips and tongue were on fire on Rafe's mouth from longing. That man could kiss!

Rafe moved his tongue to Pierce's cheek where he felt the roughness of a growing beard and licked up to the temple where he placed a kiss with his wet lips. Pierce closed his eyes and groaned. He continued his tongue's journey to Pierce's ear and he sucked on his lobe, licking the neck behind it.

His man tasted damn good. He couldn't wait to taste the rest of him. At that thought, his penis pushed against his briefs. He wanted to fuck him so badly, he didn't know how he was going to hold all the desire any longer.

Chapter 25
Pierce

t first, Pierce felt peculiar when Rafe started navigating other parts of his body with his tongue—especially his ear, of all places. He'd been kissed in a few spots while making out, but never there, never like that. He'd never gone sexual with anyone; it was always tender making out he was after, always too scared to move to something more erotic. His family had definitely done a number on him if, in his twenties, he still hadn't done foreplay, let alone fucked someone. It was always a nudging at the back of his brain, every time he kissed a guy he really liked, an activity he enjoyed so much. It would tell him that he and what he was doing

were wrong, that being so intimate with another man was inappropriate. Sinful.

They'd done a number on him, all right. He always ran off with guilt overpowering his emotions, making him feel gross, disgusting. It was exactly the same every time he'd try to beat off on his own, watching porn or fantasizing about the hottest guy in school or college, and the minute he'd reach the absolute pleasure, absolute depression deprived him of lasting feelings of happiness. He would want to wash, brush his teeth, rip his skin off, get the sin off him as if it was a disease and he was a snake that could shed it. But the craving never went away, only became stronger, as did his thoughts, preventing him from ever moving forward with anyone.

It was cute in high school when being with someone sexually meant doing something unthinkable. It was okay for the straight kids to step up their relationships, but for kids like him? Holding hands and sneaking kisses past the parents was the deal. And it was cute, despite the urges creeping up every time his skin touched foreign skin. But when he got to college? Holding hands was flirting and first date was sucking cock in the public restrooms.

All this, all these past experiences faded when he sensed Rafe's breath in his ear and his tongue wetted him. His temples pulsed and his erection begged for release from the prison of his zipper. As if knowing what he was feeling, Rafe bent down and rubbed his body on Pierce's, their cocks grinding next to each other, separated by layers of clothing that were so unnecessary he wanted to tear them apart, burn them into ashes and never again be encaged in anything but Rafe's steaming body.

And as if having Rafe on top of him working his magic wasn't enough, Rafe's tongue continued its journey down his neck. And as pleasing as having his ear sucked was, goosebumps traveled from his collarbone to the rest of his body. Rafe didn't stop there. He started placing wet kisses on his chest until his teeth gripped on his right nipple. A sharp pain shot through him and impaled his dick with an unquenchable thirst to come. And Rafe had no mercy; his hand found its way to his crotch and massaged his dick with his palm while the other hand played with his unoccupied nipple, twisting it with his fingers.

Pierce couldn't hold it anymore. His throat was dry. He was doing his best to keep the gasps inside, but the further south Rafe went, the stronger his insides trembled. He let out a loud moan as Rafe left a trail with his tongue, sucking on his belly button and licking at the top of his pubes protruding from his trousers. Rafe unbuttoned his jeans and pulled them off slowly. He threw them over his shoulder and hunched back down, biting on Pierce's cock through his briefs. Pierce panted. What the fuck was he doing? He was going to come before they'd even started.

"Fuck, you're so good," Pierce groaned, surprised his voice had any vibrato when his mouth felt so coarse.

Rafe chuckled. "You ain't felt nothing yet, *cariño*," he said and then pulled on the elastic of Pierce's underwear and placed his tongue on Pierce's bouncy dick. "Someone's happy to see me," he said, and put his lips around the erect penis, pulling the skin down with his fingers, the head of Pierce's cock immediately salivated inside Rafe's warm mouth. Pierce let out another groan with a "Fuck" escaping his lips.

On one hand he was wondering why he'd never done that before, but, on the other hand, he was glad he had saved himself for Rafe, because it made him love him even more, going the next step with the guy he loved. And he did love Rafe. It was impossible not to. They'd been through so much together in the past three months, he couldn't imagine where and what he'd be without him.

The thought of Rafe's kindness was cut

short when he felt his shaft being swallowed up, Rafe's nose touching his pelvis. Rafe moaned, and the vibrations around his penis made Pierce gasp. Rafe pulled the dick out of his mouth and tried again, tightening his lips as he sucked with much more vigor. Pierce felt the blood boiling in his groin, heat pinching at the top of his urethra, his semen begging to shoot. Pierce put his hand on the back of Rafe's head and pulled on his short hair. His dick felt cool when Rafe took it out of his mouth.

"I'm gonna come," Pierce whispered.

Rafe sat up and moaned. He took hold of Pierce's cock, rubbing it gently, his thumb pressing at the top of his head. He fell on top of Pierce and kissed his mouth, his breath a fire that burned Pierce's senses. Rafe was still stroking the dick with his right hand, the left placed next to Pierce's head, supporting him over Pierce and giving enough space between them for the handiwork.

Pierce couldn't stand seeing Rafe with his shirt still on, so he took it off for him. "You're so fucking hot."

Rafe smiled and got back to business. He whispered in Pierce's ear. "I want you to come, come right now, *cariño*," he said.

Pierce wanted to hold it longer, he didn't want to last so little, but his entire body was shaking. Desire was dribbling from his pores, and the feeling of Rafe's lips back on his mouth weakened him. His load shot between them, sprinkling Rafe's stomach and his. Rafe gasped.

He took his hand off Pierce's wet dick and unzipped his pants. He whipped his dick out. It was red and throbbing. He stroked it quickly and panted, and surely, not too many seconds later, another hot load doused them both. Rafe let out a long sigh and fell on top of Pierce's right side, their mixed come daubing their stomachs. Rafe came back for a softer, much more relaxed, kiss.

"That was…" Pierce started to say, but he didn't know if he could describe what had just happened with anything other than the three words he'd been holding on the tip of his mouth for what seemed an eternity.

"I love you," he whispered and wagged his nose with Rafe's.

Rafe lifted his head and stared at Pierce, his lids heavy over his brown eyes. He blinked and breathed on his face, but he didn't speak. Had he made a mistake? Had he just fucked everything up by saying the three formidable words that everyone seemed to always be so afraid of?

"Uh—" He opened his mouth to apologize or take it back, although taking such words back felt like the biggest sin he could ever commit.

Rafe's fingers touched his lips and shushed him. "I love you too," he said in a long sigh, taking pleasure curling the words in his mouth.

Pierce smiled. Rafe smiled. He now knew why he'd never been able to shake the guilt off of him when he'd tried to be with other guys. It wasn't his Christian background or the strict parenthood he had endured or the fate of his beloved gramps and what his family had done to him. No. The guilt had been there because his soul couldn't allow anyone else touching what was rightfully and universally Rafe's. Only Rafe made him feel at peace with himself.

Rafe. His soulmate.

Chapter 26
Pierce

Pierce woke up with a craving for Rafe's lips and good coffee. He got them both before leaving the apartment for another day of hunting real life snapshots. Rafe had worked a double the day before and was off today, so Pierce wanted to let him rest for the morning, especially after working him up overtime. They'd both slept after they'd finished, and Pierce couldn't remember a time when he'd slept better.

A shower the next morning was much needed, and when he came out, Wang was standing in the living room, staring at Pierce's naked body. Pierce tightened the towel around his hips and greeted the old man.

He was a Chinese guy with salt-and-pepper short hair and a skinny, creased face. He was wearing a marshmallow-colored shirt and black trousers, a man in his late fifties, and it showed in everything on him, even the way he breathed.

"Who are you?" he asked Pierce with a soft accent and a high pitch.

Pierce giggled and tiptoed closer to Rafe's bedroom. "I'm Rafe's friend. Remember me, Mr. Wang? I was here when Rafe moved in," he said, clutching on the door knob, ready to dive in the safety of the bedroom when given the chance.

"What are you doing here? Where is Rafe?" he asked, the cringe in his face staying there with the accompaniment of a frown.

"I slept over. I hope that's okay. Rafe is sleeping. He was working all day yesterday," Pierce explained.

Wang looked around the flat slowly. He turned to Pierce with the same expression, which seemed to be pinched on his face permanently now. "Tell Rafe I want to talk to him when he wakes up."

Uh-oh! Pierce was praying to whatever God existed at this particular moment that Wang just wanted to catch up on Rafe's life and not tell him off for bringing overnight guests.

"Actually, I'm just popping out and I don't want to wake him. He's really tired. I'm sure he'll be up by noon, though," he said.

"Okay," was all Wang responded, and Pierce found it the right moment to retreat back into the room and get dressed, trying not to make too much noise. Whatever Wang wanted with Rafe, he wasn't going to wake up his baby. Rafe needed his sleep, and Pierce needed to get out.

He put a kiss on his lover's lips and left the apartment with his suitcase and camera in hand. He hadn't had the time to fix his suitcase yet, only managed to tape it together, but he needed to take something with him to show he was leaving and wouldn't cause further problems. He felt Wang's eyes pinned to his back as he made his way across the hallway and out the door.

When he left the building, he was greeted with a sunny glare and a cool air, a combo that he wasn't sure he liked. Sun had its way of fooling you into thinking it was hot when, in fact, it was just the same old shit with sunshine rained upon it. Thankfully, it hadn't snowed yet, and Pierce hoped it wouldn't. Instead of worrying of what might happen, he decided to explore the streets of Brooklyn.

He felt like a homeless tracker pro. He could find his way to anything that was even in the slightest bit being inhabited by a street-person. He felt like the odd one out asking permission to take their pictures, when only a few weeks ago, he would have been in his natural habitat.

He tried to explain who he was and what his situation was, although the latter seemed to be problematic. He wasn't sure if he was homeless or not anymore. He was unemployed again, which sucked balls, but hopefully either Vance or Sam could take him back one way or the other or refer him to other friends. But his housing status was unclear. On one hand, he did not have a house, room, or bed that was his own, but on the other, he had spent more than two weeks in Rafe's apartment, and it felt natural being there with him, especially now that all the tension had been released and they were an item.

Eventually, he stopped explaining himself. He couldn't. But he started talking to the people and asking them what they felt like, how they became homeless, what they did before. Half of them had been normal people with addictions hadthat cost them family, friends, and possessions, and the other half had been hit by a series of unfortunate events that led up to the culmination of their homelessness. Some were gay. They couldn't hide it even if they wanted to. But there were more ambiguous identities than the gays and the lesbians. There were two trans kids whose parents had abused them or kicked them out. A gay kid whose dad had sexually harassed him for years. There was an intersex person whose parents had sent them to therapy camps, and when they remained vigorous on who they were, they were left out on their own. One kid's parents had actually moved out of their house without telling their daughter and left her to find an empty apartment when she got back from school. She had no clue where they'd gone.

Those stories were wilder than any fiction, and Pierce wasn't sure what to do with them. He scribbled some of them down; some he didn't have to. He was sure they'd haunt him for a lifetime. But even with that, he was annoyed he couldn't help. He was disturbed that all he could tell them was to hang on and to keep fighting. His only sage advice to the young ones was to clean up and try to get a job in Manhattan, but even that felt ironic when himself had only managed to do so after forty or so places and had gotten a job with a crazy guy because Vance *was* crazy. Good, but certainly not your normal boss. Knowing him now, it didn't surprise him he had hired Pierce after confronting him. But not every homeless person was Pierce, and not every boss was Vance.

He didn't promise them anything. He promised himself, leaving each and every one to their fate, that he'd find a way to help—if not them, the ones that would come after them, because he knew there would be more. Who said the world was getting more accepting? Just because the Supreme Court had legalized gay marriage across the nation didn't mean the brains, thoughts, morals, and workings of its people changed with it. If anything, those people who spewed their intolerance left and right were getting more vocal, more infectious, even.

After noon had passed, he received a message from Rafe telling him a good morning and another I love you, but when Pierce replied, his phone remained silent. He was probably busy talking to Wang about whatever it was he wanted to talk about. He was staring at his black and white phone screen, about two blocks from the flat, when he caught the leftovers of a conversation.

"I'm telling you man. Facebook is da shit these days. You wanna make money? You Facebook it. You wanna start a business? You Facebook it. You wanna say your penny of a thought? You Facebook it. Everyone's on fucking Facebook nowadays," the guy was saying to his friend, a couple walking in front of Pierce.

The other guy started to dispute the validity of his friend's words, but Pierce's brain had already lit up. He used to have a Facebook page, but when no one had been there for him when he needed a bed, a couch, a chair to sleep on, when no one had gotten back to him, he had deactivated it. But now he thought it was time to turn it back on again. Perhaps by talking to his "friends" about the situation in the streets, he'd change their minds. Make them more generous. More open. More helpful. And why lie to himself? Maybe actually get someone to see his pictures and make some money. Perhaps a newspaper would want to write an article about homelessness in America and want to use his picture to publish with it. The possibilities were endless. He had to try.

He found an internet cafe inside a convenience store and logged into his account. He was welcomed back onto the website and was hit by the pompous newsfeed of his buddies' self-indulgence. He connected the SD card to the computer and loaded up his favorite photos from that day on his wall with a few words about some of the people on the pictures. Not long after he posted an album of ten pictures, he got two likes and a comment.

"Those are incredible and heart-wrenching. Make a Page and put them up. That way more people will see them," a girl named Tanya Kosowski said.

He didn't know her. She was one of those people you added when you first created an account and found random people to boost your friendship count. He might not have known her, but he followed her suggestion almost instantly.

A half hour later, his phone buzzed, but he ignored it, his mind too occupied by his current activity to be distracted.

He finished uploading the same pictures he'd posted on his own wall, only he'd made a separate post for each of them with the stories of the people attached to them. He wrote them like eulogies, as if they'd already died, not because he wished it upon the subjects of the photographs, but because he felt that they were all doomed, and perhaps if people saw how doomed they really were they'd help more profoundly.

Only when he hit Post to the last upload, did he check his phone. He got a text from Rafe.

What time are you coming? the message read.

On my way now. Did you talk with Wang? Pierce messaged back.

Pierce paid for his time on the computer and left the store. The reply came in a single word that almost gave Pierce a heart attack.

Yes.

Chapter 27
Rafe

Pierce was back at the apartment in less than ten minutes, and Rafe was thankful; he wanted to get the problem out of the way as soon as possible and move on. He was still trying to calm his nerves when Pierce returned, and seeing him helped. Wang had locked himself in his bedroom as if nothing had happened, and Rafe pulled Pierce into his own room to talk to him. Pierce seemed agitated. Perhaps he could see the frustration in Rafe's face.

"What's going on, baby?" he asked, and Rafe's heart skipped a beat.

He still couldn't get over the fact that they were finally together. What a great night they'd had last night! He also couldn't believe that the magic of their first time had to be overshadowed by yet another problem in their happy ever after, but he guessed they might as well get that out of their way before moving forward with their lives once and for all.

"I spoke with Wang," Rafe started, "and he wasn't happy that I invited you over for the holidays. And I explained that you were in an accident and all, but now he's saying that if you don't leave then *I* can't stay here anymore either." He tried to speak as slowly as he could to soften the blow, but it still hit Pierce hard. He took a seat, clutching his stomach, and stared at the floor rather than his boyfriend.

"God! I'm so sorry, Rafe." And there it was: the guilt pouring out of him as it had before. The sulking and the blame all mixed into his voice and his body language. "I didn't mean to cause trouble. I thought you'd told him, and… Anyway, it doesn't matter. I'll take my stuff and go. I wouldn't wanna—" he continued, but Rafe couldn't let him finish that sentence.

That guy. That fucking guy. Pierce would do everything for him and he knew all he needed from the sentence he didn't let Pierce finish. Pierce would sacrifice his own health and safety to keep Rafe out of harm's way. He would return to the streets rather than have Rafe homeless and unmedicated. That was one of the thousand reasons why Rafe loved him. Yet he was failing to realize that they were a couple now, and they would face their problems together.

"Pierce." He knelt next to him. "don't blame yourself. That guy is a douchebag. A heartless douchebag. I mean, who does that? Who kicks two sick guys out of his house? Don't take this on your shoulders," he told him, massaging his knee, trying to find Pierce's eyes, which were lost somewhere in the empty space.

Pierce closed his eyes and shook his head. Moments later he got up with a look of strain and pain in his face and got a couple books from the shelf above the bed, then zipped up the wardrobe and started to stuff his countless shirts into a small bag.

"What do you think you're doing?" Rafe asked.

Pierce didn't stop. He didn't look at Rafe either. "I'm gonna go. Like I said, I'm sorry for ruining your life," he mumbled.

"Ruin—" Rafe tried to say the word but choked on its hardness. He grabbed Pierce's arm and stopped him. He got in front of him and put both his hands on Pierce's cheeks, then looked straight into the abyss of his eyes. "You. Gave. Me. My. Life. Back. Never say that you ruined it ever again. Okay?"

Pierce's eyes turned red and the tears started falling, wetting Rafe's palms. "What do you even want with me? I destroy everything I touch. I'm a nobody," he sobbed.

Rafe couldn't help feeling like wrapping his arms around him and smacking him in the head, both at the same time. That guy. He was fucking clueless. "You are my world," he said, making sure every word made an impact on him.

"No. I make this world cruel with my presence. That's why nobody wants me around. That's why my parents kicked me out. That's why Vance sent me away—" he kept muttering to himself.

Rafe shook Pierce's head to bring his attention back to him. "Listen to me, you *idiota*. Anyone who wants you out of their life, doesn't deserve you in it. Because you make this world a sweeter, more beautiful place. You make my life better. You make my life worth living. Crappy life has given us each other, and I don't know if you've noticed, but we make a fucking good team. So stop beating yourself, put your things back where they were, and sit down. Because you are going nowhere. Okay? If someone has to leave this place it will both of us. Together. Okay?" He shouted at him and his own eyes stung, but he didn't care now. All he wanted was to get Pierce to stop.

And he did. He stopped crying and kissed Rafe. It was a salty kiss, but it was their strongest yet.

The both sat on the bed and Rafe wiped both their eyes before continuing. "So since the dickhead wants us out, I thought maybe it was time we went with our initial plan and found a place together."

"That sounds good," Pierce whispered, and chuckled when Rafe rolled his eyes. "I'm sorry. I guess I'm a drama queen," he apologized.

"Oh, *cariño*, you're the biggest one of all."

They kissed again and this time they both felt calm.

"How are we going to afford it, though? Last time you didn't have a job and it was a pain in the butt. Now I don't have a job and I doubt things in the market have changed in the last couple of months," Pierce asked, seemingly ready to deal with reality.

Rafe shrugged. "We'll figure it out. Okay? We still have some time. He gave us to the end of the month. So we'll figure something out," he added.

Pierce nodded but didn't seem so sure. Rafe wasn't sure himself how they were gonna deal with the paperwork, and all the crap that came with looking for a room, but he wouldn't stress about it right at this moment. He preferred to spend some quality time with his boyfriend than worry about tomorrow. Stress would solve nothing. Plus he was working the next day; he could ask for the sage advice of Vance. He might have a solution. The important thing was that he and Pierce stuck together. They could conquer the world if they were. And that was what he wanted Pierce to see. That they were better together than apart.

Chapter 28
Rafe

afe sliced the orange peel and squeezed it over the glass, then dropped the twist into the Cosmopolitan. He put the glass on the tray with the others and started the next ticket. It was Friday night at Les Fourches, and the place was packed with people dining or wining. He was on bar duty today. Vance had told him he was thinking of promoting Rafe to supervisor now that the old one was leaving, and he was working so many more hours a week he'd had no time to look for an apartment with Pierce, who was still resting at home and doing his morning photographic sessions routine.

He was good. He was getting better and grungier day by day, and he loved what he was doing. He spent the afternoons uploading pictures on Facebook and his evenings reading books or viewing apartments. It had been two weeks, however, and they'd had no luck with their search.

It was like November all over again, only this time they didn't have the funds to actually move into any apartment, despite having a guarantor in Vance. One would think with Rafe's overtime he'd have a small fortune saved by now, but they'd had no such luck. They still had to pay Wang and their bills. Uncle Sam was being a pain in the butt the more hours Rafe worked, and dealing partially with Pierce's hospital bills, it was all in the way of finding a new house. He was basically working for two people, and the money wasn't enough. Even the tips didn't help. With the Christmas spirit emptier than ever, people went back to their stingy selves, and business had dropped during the week, so anything Rafe managed to make was during the coveted weekend. Vance had to drop three staff members—who had only been hired for the season anyway—so that meant Rafe had longer but less-rewarding work days. Hopefully he'd get the supervisor position soon enough, because it came with a pay raise, and he sure could do with that.

Not that he was complaining. Three months ago he'd had nothing. He had no job, no house, no friends, no family. Now he had it all. So what if it came with a few roadblocks? They were part of life, right? Whenever he'd dream before he had anything, having everything had meant waving goodbye to unnecessary drama and problems. But that wasn't realistic, and he was only beginning to realize now that he didn't care. As long as he had Pierce, everything was manageable. As long as they had each other, they would brave the storms.

His phone vibrated in his back pocket. These days he kept his phone on him in case Pierce had an emergency or found a room and needed to check if Rafe would be free to look at it. He still hadn't fully recovered from the attack and still had trouble getting up and sitting down or doing extremely physical things. But day by day he was getting better.

He stopped pouring a beer and checked his screen quickly. It wasn't Pierce. It was an unknown number. And the time was two a.m. He wanted to pick it up, but the place was still buzzing with life and disorder. He looked at his colleague who was busy serving people at the bar and tried to get his attention.

"Can—can I get this real quick? I'll only

be a minute," he whispered in his ear.

His colleague nodded but wasn't too happy being left to deal with the entire place on his own. Rafe couldn't do anything about it, though. The more his phone rang, the more worried he got. By the time he reached the back and entered the staff room, his phone had stopped ringing. He called Pierce. He usually picked up by the third ring, but this time he didn't. He let it go to voicemail and hung up. Now he was really worried.

He found the number that had just called him and rang it back. In a second it was answered, and his knees gave up on him. He collapsed on the sofa. "St. Andrew Hospital, how may I help?"

His mouth felt dry all of a sudden and his throat was hoarse. When his voice finally came out, it was stale and barely audible. "Hi, I just missed a call from you. Can you tell me what this is about?"

"What's your name, sir?" the woman asked on her phone.

"It's Rafael Arena Santos," he replied.

She was quiet. Rafe kept quiet too. He was praying it was a mistake, that nothing had happened.

"Ah, there it is. Yes, I called you because your friend Pierce Callahan has been admitted in the ER, and you are his emergency contact," she said.

Rafe's heart nearly ripped his skin apart, and he gasped deeply to find the courage to ask what was happening. "Is he okay? What happened? When was he admitted?"

The woman typed something and answered. "His wound has been infected, and he was found by a homeless man passed out on Nassau Avenue. The man said he found his phone and called us because he wouldn't wake up. He was brought in an hour ago," she said.

"What—what was he doing in the street? What time did they find him?"

"We do not know that. He was found around midnight. Do you think you can come around? We don't know when he will be out of the ER, but I'm sure he could use a friend," she said.

Rafe got up and started fumbling with his locker, trying to get his bag out. "But is he going to be okay?"

"Like I said, sir, we don't know for sure when he will be out, but the infection doesn't seem to be life-threatening. The doctors are waiting for his response to the medication to have a better picture of your friend's condition."

Rafe nodded, said he was making his way over, and hung up. Next thing on his mission was finding Vance and telling him what had happened. He couldn't possibly stay at work and finish his shift when Pierce was fighting for his life.

He found him in the empty kitchen, nibbling on some salad. Rafe choked on his words, trying to tell him he had to leave and the reason why. Vance put his salad down and gave Rafe a warm hug. His arms felt good around him. Fatherly almost, he would dare say, if he knew what a fatherly touch was. Vance reassured him that everything would be okay then took his position behind the bar and took over for him. Rafe called a cab and rode it all the way to Brooklyn and St. Andrew Hospital.

When he got there, they told him Pierce was responding to the drugs and would be out within the hour. Rafe tried to sit down while he was waiting for the minutes to tick by, but he couldn't. He was pacing the corridor, each time covering longer distances until he ended up in the hospital cafeteria and grabbed a sandwich, which he ate in minutes and only because he needed to put something in his stomach, even though nothing seemed to be going down easily. He ate so fast, nothing tasted of anything.

At four a.m. Pierce was taken to a room, and Rafe sat down on the chair and finally got to nap a little after a long day, made longer by what had happened. Even sleep couldn't let him find peace for long, and he woke up at five, then again at six. At nine, when he opened his eyes, Pierce was awake and watching the TV.

"Hey," Rafe said and got up to touch Pierce and give him a kiss.

Pierce didn't respond.

"What happened last night? How did you end up on Nassau?" Rafe inquired, his voice gentle, trying not to be too loud or intrusive. Although being considerate of the other patients in the room wasn't on top of his list when his boyfriend was suffering.

"I'm sorry," he groaned.

Rafe winced and asked for an explanation.

"I gave up on us. I'm sorry. I couldn't take seeing you overwork yourself for my sake. I've literally seen you one full day since Wang told you I can't stay there anymore. You just come home to sleep for a few hours and go back to work, and I just couldn't stand seeing you like that. You're unhappy. You need a break," he said.

Rafe grabbed Pierce's chin and turned his boyfriend's head around to face him. "What are you talking about?"

Pierce closed his eyes before he continued. He sighed. "I decided to leave. Go back to the streets, so you don't have to move out," he said.

"What? Why? What about all the things we talked about?"

Pierce opened his eyes and looked directly at Rafe. "Well, now that I've left, you don't have to work for the two of us. I've seen you go from a happy-go-lucky guy to a man who can't even smile anymore without forcing it. This whole ordeal is making you unhappy, and I don't wanna be the reason for that. That's why I left," he explained.

Rafe didn't say anything. He whacked Pierce across the head, infection or not. "My God! I *am* actually dating an *estúpido*. I'm not unhappy. I'm just tired. But I didn't care because at the end of the day I slept next to you, even if only for a few hours, and having that, I could wrestle fucking lions the next day. Because I had you. Do you not remember what I told you that day that Wang was kicking us out? Don't you? Do you think I am that feeble to take it all back, or that my feelings aren't strong enough to last through a hardship?"

Pierce tried to say something, but Rafe didn't let him.

"And what is wrong with you? You're acting like you don't want to do better in life. Like you've made up your mind that you are homeless and that you're going to be for the rest of your life, despite the fact that so many opportunities have come your way to prove to you that you *can* get over this. I thought you loved me and you wanted to be with me."

"I do," Pierce hesitated before he interrupted Rafe. "I do love you. I do want to be with you," he added.

"Then prove it," he shouted. Rafe was raging and he didn't care one bit. He loved Pierce, but he was so annoyed he was having his doubts about whether he truly felt the same. "Prove to me that you do, because I am seriously *this* close to walking away from whatever *this*—" he shook his arms around them two—"is supposed to be. Because until a few minutes ago I thought *this*—" he repeated the same action—"was a relationship."

Pierce was biting his lip and looking at the sheets covering him. He didn't dare to look at Rafe, and it was making him even more furious. He growled, then turned around and picked up his jacket, ready to leave. He was so blinded by his anger that at the moment he didn't care what happened to Pierce unless he showed the same willingness to commit to their relationship.

"I'm an idiot," he cried and stopped Rafe from turning the latch and opening the door. "Don't go. Please."

Rafe didn't move. He couldn't decide if he could trust Pierce's words anymore. He seemed to be using them sparingly but without any real emotion. He needed proof. He told Pierce so without turning his head, still staring at the door.

"I don't know how. I don't know how to stop you from going away. I do love you, and I don't know what's so fucked up with me that I can't see that you do too. I will understand if you go. It will break my heart, but I will understand it. I'm not an easy person to be with. I think my parents fucked me up more than I realize. But that's no excuse. So if you have to go, go. The only thing I can think of to convince you to stay is to tell you 'please take me home'."

The room went quiet. The patients that were awake were all surely looking at Rafe, because he could feel their prying eyes burning his back. Even the noise of the TV in the back of the room seemed to mute itself in anticipation for Rafe's response. He was so sick of words, of Pierce's words. Of Pierce realizing his stupidity and apologizing. Of Pierce throwing sorries around like they were cookies. But damn it if he'd walk away from him when he was begging him to take him home.

"Okay, *estúpido*," he said and turned around.

Like he had guessed, everyone was looking at him. And Pierce was too. And he was crying. He was a fucking mess. But Rafe loved that mess with all his heart. He covered the few steps between them and took his hands. He kissed him. The other people in the room made their existence known by fawning over them, and both Rafe and Pierce, without breaking their kiss, looked at them.

Yes, they were going home. And home was wherever each other was. Even if that meant they were both back in the streets and sleeping in subway trains.

Chapter 29
Pierce

Pierce woke up and, before doing anything else, changed his bandages. Coffee was next on the list.

He wanted to go out for another photographic session, but the place was a mess and needed a tidy-up, so he spent the next hour doing that. It was surprising how much time cleaning a tiny space consumed. He put his and Rafe's clothes in the washer and put the clean ones back in the wardrobe. Changed the sheets for new ones and put Rafe's growing sketchbook collection in order. Then he dusted, cleaned the window, and vacuumed.

Rafe had already left for work. He had forgiven Pierce so quickly, but Pierce hadn't done so yet himself. Everything Rafe had told him at the hospital was true, and he couldn't stop beating himself up for making Rafe hurt so much with his reckless actions. He wasn't going to do anything similar again. He had learned his lesson.

He never wanted to break what he had with Rafe; he never even wanted to put it at risk. He did what he did to make life easier for Rafe. Sure, they'd agreed to go on together, but when he kept seeing Rafe's mood declining, his work hours increasing, and his sleep time reducing, he couldn't help but feel guilty. Rafe was also a sick man, despite his medication, and Pierce's condition was putting extra stress on him. All he thought of every time Rafe got back home and dropped on the bed to sleep was that he was making him feel sick again. He felt like a burden to his own boyfriend because he felt like a burden to himself. He hated that he couldn't get back to work yet. Vance had agreed to take Pierce back part-time when he was ready, but that wouldn't be for another month, if his brash behavior hadn't pulled an extension on his recovery.

He still couldn't lift things, bend down or kneel. Walking helped. It was everything else that was a struggle. His medication was strong and wore him out quicker. Sometimes when he complained about being tired to Rafe he felt egocentric, compared to Rafe's exhaustion. Not that he wasn't happy with his baby's development in the restaurant. He wished he could be there with him, working with him and helping with their situation. He felt like an imposter that had been given all this spare time with nothing to spend it on but taking pictures.

So that was why he'd run away. He wanted his baby to be fine and well, even if it meant he wouldn't, that they'd be apart. He was trying to help. Of course looking back now, not even five days later, he wanted to hang himself for his idiocy. However, he was sure if he tried, Rafe would find a way to revive him and kill him with his own hands.

It did seem as if he had a death wish. Every time things got rough, he wanted to run away, and then he would complain that his life was going nowhere. His life *would* go nowhere if he kept running, and he understood that the moment Rafe nearly walked out on him. Leaving him to have a better life was hard, and he was sure he would manage the pain, but Rafe walking out on him, not loving him anymore—he wasn't sure he could handle that. He did want to do better in life. He was sure that meant being with Rafe. He just needed a constant reminder. A constant reminder that he was worth as much as Rafe said he was, and that he was loved and needed as much as he loved and needed Rafe.

He finished with the room and had something quick to eat. He felt very dirty after cleaning the room, even though it hadn't been too dusty. But he couldn't have a shower, as much as he wanted to. His wound still hurt like a motherfucker, and he needed help getting in and out, even turning was a strain, so whenever he needed a shower, he did it with Rafe. He couldn't complain. It made the process much more fun. It made him forget the pain.

The doctors had prescribed him such strong medication to battle the infection and to ease the pain that he couldn't go longer than four hours without a nap. He wanted to go back to the streets with his camera, though. He couldn't wait any longer. The last three days locked in the room had been horrifying. The room was starting to feel smaller and asphyxiating. He needed fresh air and another reminder that there was something he was good at. He would just have to do a short session around the neighborhood and return home before he fainted in public.

It was ten when he looked at the clock, so he told himself he had to be back by twelve, nap, and then go view a room.

That was another issue. The month was running out and people were coming to view the room that Rafe and Pierce slept in, even while they were actually sleeping. Wang didn't even bother asking them anymore, nor knocking. That's why they made sure to lock the door until morning. Rafe couldn't even talk to Wang anymore. His crappy behavior made his eyes twitch and his fists curl.

So they only had a little under two weeks left until February, and no agent would let them rent anything. Even though Pierce had a few pay stubs to show them and Vance ensuring he'd be back to work soon, and despite that fact he was also willing to be their guarantor. The private landlords were not trusting either. Pierce had called every ad he'd found online, even viewed a couple of rooms that were smaller than Rafe's current one that were completely uninhabitable. They had viewed some rooms that were pretty nice, had even viewed a studio on the North edge of the city that was almost in their price range. It had been divine, ideal, but the agent wouldn't even discuss it with Pierce and Rafe if they didn't have all that they asked for.

He was going to be calling a few more private landlords later today. He'd found a few rooms that were cheaper, and if they really *were* cheaper, then they could probably convince the owner they could afford it. The good thing was that with the Christmas season officially over, accommodations were emptying up and there were more popping up every day online. Hopefully, they would find something before their time was up.

Pierce returned to the room and looked for his camera, and despite the very few places it could be, he couldn't find it anywhere.

He had left it for Rafe when he'd decided to leave. He hadn't thought he deserved his gift anymore and thought that perhaps he could sell it back. But now that he was in his right mind, he wanted it, couldn't imagine going through his recovery without it.

"Where did Rafe put you, for fuck's sake?" he cursed and kicked the bed.

Only it wasn't the bed he kicked, but his suitcase, and the motion hurt his stomach so much that he curled up on the end of the bed, where he tried to control the pain. He looked on the floor at his broken suitcase. It still hadn't been fixed, and kicking it had sent the top flap flying to the wall. Inside the suitcase was his camera case.

"That's where he put you," he said to the camera.

The pain backed away and he sat up on the bed, taking the case out of the suitcase and putting it next to him on the bed. Then, carefully, he leaned forward and lifted the top part of the suitcase to his lap. He looked at the hinges and the nails that had been keeping it together. They were completely gone. He turned it in his hands, looking to see if it was salvageable with superglue. But instead of answering the question to his curiosity, his curiosity was piqued by a tear in the lining. He cursed.

He pulled the torn lining and cussed again when, without meaning to, he pulled more fabric out of its stitches. Before he could slap himself, an envelope held his attention. It was there, behind the lining, waiting for Pierce. Had it been there all along, or was it something someone put there recently, the reason why the lining was torn? The envelope had soaked up the dyes of the suitcase and was almost yellow. But it surely couldn't be that old. He would have noticed the envelope moving behind the lining, or the outline of it every time he opened the suitcase.

He shook his head and pulled the envelope out. It hadn't been glued shut, so he opened it and pulled out some papers. One was a letter. He unfolded it and read.

Pierce, my dear boy,
I am writing this letter in case I never
get the chance to tell you in person
and, considering how your parents
have been treating me, I doubt I will

be able to. I hope you find this letter sooner rather than later, but I had to conceal it so that your parents don't get a hold of it and dispose of it. Hopefully, that is not what happens. Hopefully, they have not broken the lock. Hopefully, my suitcase will reach you when you are well into your adulthood and I will have had some more years to my life, but since my health has taken its toll, I would rather be safe than sorry.

My dear boy, as you may know, I am a homosexual man. You have probably learnt to associate this word with the Devil. For heaven's sake, in our family it is worse being homosexual than a witch. But I wanted you to know that I am not a pervert, and I did not abandon my family because I was brainwashed. Your parents might have told you that I was an evil man, but I am not. I promise I am not. Your grandma did not think so. Surely, it took her some time, but in the end she contacted me and told me she forgave me, and understood why I did what I did. She even said she had an inkling even before I had.

So as you already know, I left your grandma and my children. That is what your dad told you, did he not? The truth is I *did not want to. I wanted to stay, be part of your lives, but he and your uncle could not grasp the idea that their beloved father was a queer. Pardon my language, but be assured they used far meaner words to describe and insult their own father than that word. Queer almost blurs in comparison. They told me they did not want me to be around them anymore, spreading my sickness to their families. So I left, and I had no one. At the time, your grandma was still not talking to me. I took whatever I had and traveled. It was a wonderful experience. I learnt more about being true to myself than that darn church ever taught me. I met people from all walks of life. I learnt not to judge, just like I did not want others to judge me. My trips were a revelation. Being a homosexual, a gay man, is more than the sin those religious idiots I call my children preach about. Being gay means to be happy, yet so many people have tried to make me unhappy. I know now that being gay runs within me and I could not have changed it no matter how many women I slept with, or how many confessions I went through.*

Being gay is wonderful. Being part of a loving community. And we do have our community. I made friends I never thought I would. They were there for me in my darkest of moments, and my happiest. I have made some close friendships. I have even found a partner. Who? Me. A 71-year-old bag like me. His name is Roland, and he is 75. We have both been married, had families, then accepted who we are. The only difference is his family still talks to him. And they have welcomed me into their house. They even call me dad. Huh, would you believe that? I am a happy man. I no longer living a lie. Trust me; It's amazing to live your life truthfully. I only wish it did not mean being away from you.

Now, you might be wondering why I might be telling you all this. Well, the first reason is because I wanted to explain myself, my disappearance. I wanted you to know the truth, in my own words and not the filtered lies you might have heard from your family. I wanted you to know that I love you very much and that I am very proud of you. To me, you are twice my son. I know you loved me too. I hope that did not change when your parents fed you with their lies. If you still love your old grandpa, know I am happy.

Pierce wiped a tear from his eye and sniffed in the snot that threatened to come out of his nose.

He hadn't talked to his grandad for years before he died. When he found out about his death, he had nearly choked. His breath had stopped. The tears he shed were unstoppable. He kept thinking how he'd missed the chance to tell him goodbye and how much he loved him. His parents would tell him that boys don't cry and that he should stop. But he couldn't. It gnawed on him that he hadn't told his grandpa he loved him. That he would never talk to him again. But now *he* was talking to Pierce. And he knew. He knew that Pierce loved him and that he didn't believe anything his parents had told him. He knew.

He wiped his eyes again and continued on the second page of the letter:

The second reason why I am telling you all this, is because I think you might be gay yourself. I have known you since you were a tiny seed in your mother's stomach, and seeing you grow up I saw so much of myself in you. You were not like all the other boys. You were not like your father or your uncle had been when they were children. You were a free spirit. You were so creative. So smart. So sweet. So gentle. When you had reached puberty I was sure — well, as sure as you can be, that you were more like me than anybody could tell. So the reason why I told you about my life is so that you know that you can live a normal life if you really are homosexual yourself. You can find happiness like I did. It is not a sin and you do not need to ask for forgiveness from anybody. You hear me?

If it was any indication from the way your parents treated me, I thought you might be struggling with the same feelings, and if you ever find the courage to tell them, know that you will always have a parent in me. That is why I wrote this letter. Hopefully, your parents change their ways, but in case they do not, know that you are loved and you are free to love whoever you want. And because I never want you to feel alone like I did when they wrote me off, I've put something in the envelope for you. That was the other reason I hid the letter. Because I did not want your parents getting a hold of it.

With love,
Your gramps Kevan Callahan

Pierce put the letter down and let himself cry. He couldn't hold it in anymore, and there was no point. Crying hurt his wound, but he couldn't stop himself. It hurt more not to.

When it was all out, he blew his nose on the napkins they kept by the bed and wiped his face. He took the envelope and the other papers that had been inside it and opened them to see what they were.

He cried again.

Chapter 30
Rafe

Bye, Rafe. Tell Pierce he better get back soon, or I'll kick his ass," Damian said as he was leaving the bar after close.

"Will do," Rafe replied.

"Good night, sweetie." Damian winked at him and made his way down the street.

Rafe had seen Damian almost every day that week. He had first met him when he got a job at Les Fourches and Pierce introduced them. Pierce had only recently told him he had made out with him. When he had next seen Damian he wanted to punch his face, but Damian was too sweet to be jealous of him. Damian himself had reassured Rafe he was no competition. Still, Rafe didn't like the idea of his man with another one, especially one so handsome.

He grabbed his rucksack from the staff room and waved the supervisor good night. Vance had the night off for a date, and Rafe couldn't wait to hear all about it.

He walked out of the restaurant and was making his way to the subway when his phone rang. When he looked at it, he saw it was Pierce. Some sense of déjà vu hit him and he didn't like it one bit. Pierce never called him this late, only texted him before going to bed.

"Hello?" he answered it as calmly as possible.

He heard Pierce on the other end. He was in pain. "Rafe. You have to come get me. I'm not feeling very well," he said.

Rafe rolled his eyes and stomped his foot on the ground. "What? Where are you?"

"I'm at Riverdale. I can text you the address, I think," he replied.

That was almost out of the city. "What the hell are you doing there, Pierce?"

He wailed before he answered Rafe's question. "I'm sorry. I—I thought I was doing something good for you."

Rafe raged inside and he wanted to tell Pierce to seriously go fuck himself, but he was in pain, and as much as he wanted to teach him another lesson, he needed to make sure he was okay first. He hailed a cab and gave the driver the address that Pierce gave him. He told Pierce to stay on the line, but Pierce hung up.

Was he trying to infuriate him? Because it was working. What the hell was he doing all the way across town and in pain? Again? Why hadn't he called 911? What was wrong with him?

He found it difficult to sit on the backseat, playing with his phone in his hands and rolling the window up and down, getting too hot one moment and too cold the next. It had only been four days since they were back from the damn hospital. Why was he running again?

They made their way through the Upper East Side and entered the Bronx. There was not much traffic. On a Tuesday night, there wasn't much traffic to contend with. When they continued all the way across the Bronx and entered the street Pierce was supposed to be at, he recognized the neighborhood. Pierce and he had viewed a house around this area not more than a week ago, two days before Pierce ran off the first time. It was one of the viewings that he had managed to go to with Pierce, and he'd regretted it.

He had fallen in love with the place. It had only been a studio, but it was on the fourth floor, had its own bathroom and kitchen, and, despite the mold on the ceiling, the old wooden cupboards in the kitchen, and the plumbing that needed changing, it was a great flat. It was a bit over their budget, at $1400 before the bills or the city tax, so convincing the agency they were able to afford it was a pain. They had to leave the viewing doubly disappointed.

The taxi stopped in front of number 107, and when the driver announced their arrival, Rafe immediately looked around, searching for Pierce in the shadows. He quickly paid the large fare with half his tips and exited the car. He looked around some more, but Pierce was nowhere. He got on the curb and looked on the ground for a body, but as far as his eyes could see there weren't any. The lights from building 107 were offering a generous amount of luminance, but Pierce was nowhere to be found.

"Rafe." He heard his voice and turned to look at the building entrance.

He had seen a man standing there when he exited the cab, but he had assumed he was the doorman. The man was tall and well-built, in a black suit with skinny trousers and a red shirt, in his hands a small bouquet of white and red roses. As he approached the man and his vision cleared from the birght lights, he saw it was Pierce, and he was smiling. He had the audacity to smile.

Rafe smacked him in the head.

"What the hell did you do again?"

Pierce laughed.

Then Rafe realized. "Wait. What are you wearing? Where did you get this?"

Pierce leaned in and whispered in his ear. "Shh."

He gave him the bouquet, took Rafe's hand, and walked him to the door. He put his free hand in the coat pocket, took a pair of keys out, and opened the door.

"Where are we going? Where did—"

Pierce shushed him again, resting his finger on Rafe's lips.

When Rafe quietened, he gave him a kiss.

"I was ready to go and shoot some pictures today when I noticed my gramps's suitcase had a tear. I found an envelope with a letter from him," he said as he walked him to the elevator.

Rafe stared at Pierce and how well he cleaned up. Not that he didn't know that already, but he'd never seen him in a suit before. He loved it, and it made his crotch awaken. His frustration dissipated. Pierce pressed the elevator button, and when the door opened he let Rafe enter first before following and pressing number four.

"In it, he told me how proud he was of his coming out and accepting himself and how much he loved me. He also told me he had a feeling I was gay too when I was growing up, and that he didn't want history to repeat itself," Pierce continued.

The elevator slowed down and Pierce propped the door open, again letting Rafe get out first. Rafe recognized the doors. He recognized the floor and now the building. It was the same building they had viewed the studio apartment. Pierce led him to the same door they'd walked through six days ago—4D.

"So in the letter he told me he opened a bank account for me and included all the details in the letter. So I visited the bank and asked to access the account." Pierce put a key in the door and opened it.

It was fully lit with fairy lights. Rafe's fairy lights that he had put on the ceiling of his room. Pierce asked him to go in first. He did. He walked through the small hallway that led to the open space kitchen and living room of the apartment. There were no couches, only a table and two chairs. There was Chinese takeaway and two glasses of wine next to a bottle of red laid out on the table, which was dressed with a white tablecloth. A few feet from the table, and against the wall, a pile of books. Pierce's pile of books. And next to it Rafe's own stack of sketchbooks.

Then he looked at the bed on the right. It was only a mattress, but it was wrapped with a beige comforter, rose petals lain in a heart shape on top of it. There were tea light candles lit everywhere. Rafe couldn't understand what was happening. Why were their things here? Even his canvas wardrobe was there next to the bed, next to Pierce's suitcase.

"What—what's all this?" he stuttered.

Pierce gave him a kiss on the cheek and took hold of both his hands. "In the bank account there was a bit over fifty grand, Rafe. My grandpa saved money for me so that I could be independent of my parents and their hatred. We are fucking rich, baby," he exclaimed.

Rafe had never seen him like that. Gone were the brusque facade and the cold eyes that only he could see through. He was like a child who had met Santa and actually got the present he'd asked for. And what a present it was. Fifty thousand wasn't a small amount of money.

"And how did this happen?" It seemed stupid of Rafe to ask, but he couldn't believe he had managed to move out in a day without Rafe knowing.

"When I saw the amount of money in it, well, I knew we were saved. We could finally get an apartment together and get out of Wang's way. So I called the agency and asked them if they still had this studio. I know how much you liked it and it was so cheap, compared to the other places, anyway. So I paid them six months in advance and *voila*—a couple taxi rides later, we're here, and *this* is all ours," he explained.

Rafe smiled and hugged Pierce. "Can't believe you did this in a day's work. Are you feeling okay? You didn't lift anything, did you?" he took Pierce's face in his hands.

Pierce shook his head. "I called Damian and he helped me out. He even bought us a housewarming present," he replied and let go of Rafe to show him a *Star Wars: The Force Awakens* clock, already pinned on the wall in the kitchen.

That bastard. He was in on the secret and he had played all innocent. No wonder he'd only come into the restaurant at ten p.m. Rafe had thought that was weird. But what did it matter now? He was with Pierce, they were out of the craphole, and they were happy. Nothing else mattered. He kissed his boyfriend with a passion he hadn't before, there in a barren house, waiting for them to fill it. They were finally free of the stress and the apartment hunts and worry and desperation. They were finally free to be happy. Fully happy. And he could feel it in the air.

Chapter 31
Pierce

hen Pierce woke up the next morning, he was surprised by the sour smell of coffee beans and a full breakfast waiting for him at the table in the living room. Rafe had already woken up and was busy in the kitchen, but when he saw Pierce get out of bed, he rushed by his side to help him up.

"What is all this?" he asked when he saw the glorious meal waiting for him on the table. On one plate were two brioche buns with spinach, tomato, avocado, and melted vegan cheese on top, pita bread with hummus, and tofu frittata. There was strawberry juice, orange juice, and in a plate in the middle were pancakes with strawberries, coconut ice cream, and maple syrup. The mixture of the smells made him salivate, and he couldn't wait to get started on them, but first he wanted to get started on Rafe himself.

"I woke up early and decided to fill up the fridge and make you some breakfast. Although I only take credit for the pancakes and the brioche. The pita bread I bought ready-made," Rafe said and returned to the kitchen, getting busy with the frying pan over the stove.

Pierce followed him and put his hands on Rafe's hips and his head on his shoulder. "What you cooking? Aren't you going to sit down with me?"

Rafe turned his head and kissed Pierce. Pierce turned him around and deepened the kiss. This guy; he was his everything.

"I'm just finishing up on the mushrooms," Rafe replied when he resurfaced from the intimacy. "I know how much you love your mushrooms in the morning."

Pierce hummed and hugged his boyfriend tight. "I love you. Have I told you that?"

"Last night, if I remember right," Rafe chuckled. "But by all means, don't stop saying it. Now go eat, before it gets cold."

Pierce sat down on the table and started on

the brioche buns. When he finished his first one, Rafe emptied the mushrooms onto both their plates and sat down with him.

"I thought I'd wake up and find out it was all a bad dream," Rafe told him.

"Me too. But it's not. I *do* have you," Pierce said and reached out for Rafe's hands.

"What are you gonna do today? I gotta go to work at five."

Pierce gazed out of the window that was right in front of the table. The sky was gray, but the glass was blurred by the fall of snowflakes. It was snowing. And he found, for the first time, that he wasn't half as mad about it as he would have been once. He still felt bad for all the people that couldn't have the kind of shelter he had. He hadn't forgotten about them in the least. He had just learned to accept his own happiness without guilt. Otherwise he wouldn't be able to help. And he still wanted to. He just hadn't found the right way to do so.

"I'm gonna stay in. I thought I might go out and buy a laptop so I don't have to go out to upload my photos," he answered to Rafe.

Rafe clapped his hands together like a six-year-old. He was adorable. "How exciting. That sounds fun. Can I come with?"

Pierce laughed. He didn't believe he even had to ask. Any moment away from Rafe was torture. He wasn't gonna deny his boyfriend and his heart, the joy of togetherness. Even though they had a whole bunch of lifetime ahead together, he didn't want to be apart from him unless absolutely necessary.

When they'd finished their breakfast, they got ready and left their house for the nearest market. The snow didn't look as it was going to settle; it was only a tender but sharp reminder of the closing season giving its finale. It was only a month before spring and Pierce couldn't wait for it. But before that, it was Valentine's, and now that he could afford it he was going to give Rafe a great present. Frankly, all he wanted to spend his newly acquired money on was on his boyfriend. He didn't much care about himself. He'd rented the house Rafe had loved and had done it for Rafe, so that he wouldn't stress and worry about anything anymore.

Pierce returned to the flat on his own since Rafe had to leave for work. Pierce had a full evening of exploring his new laptop, and when he finally logged it onto the internet with the help of mobile Wi-Fi the store-person had sold him, he grabbed his camera and decided to upload some of the pictures he had taken.

When he accessed his Facebook homepage he was struck by the red number on the top of his page. He checked the name on the profile to make sure he hadn't somehow accidentally logged into another man's account, but naturally that wasn't the case. He had 2,409 notifications, 45 messages, and 367 friend requests. He was scared to open any of them. But he eventually clicked on the notification button and was taken back by the content.

Most of it was to notify him of the number of likes on his page, Dreamless in New York, and to let him know of the targets he had reached. He'd had a little over 10,000 likes. He wasn't even able to take the number in. It had been over a week since his last login and update, yet all his posts and pictures had thousands of comments, likes, and shares. He spent an enormous chunk of time reading all the comments and clearing the rest of his notifications.

Then he got into the messages. So many of them to go through. The messages were more personal, even if he didn't know the people in question. Most of them told him how much they admired his pictures and how much his stories had touched them. Some said they wanted to help the people in the photos, and others were asking how they could do so. He found a few messages were from old friends who had heard about him and had been worried when he had deleted his Facebook page, telling him how glad they were to hear from him again and asked him about his wellbeing and his health.

And then out of all the messages, there was the one that made him rub his eyes and question his sanity.

***

Hello Mr. Pierce Callahan,

My name is Dolores Ortega and I'm sending you this personal message to make an enquiry. I saw your photographic work on your page 'Dreamless in New York' and I have to say I'm in awe of the talent and raw emotion that your pictures emanate. I have been going through them over and over again, balling my eyes out with these stories. I'm a New Yorker myself and I can't believe these brave people live in my city and I haven't even given them a second of my time before. First of all, I wanted to ask if you have set up a fundraising account where we can deposit funds to help those poor souls. If you haven't, make sure you do. I saw the interaction on your page and I believe there are others like me who want to do something about the homelessness that is tearing this city apart. Secondly, I wanted to make you, the artist, an offer. I own an art gallery in Manhattan and I wanted to ask you if you'd be willing to exhibit your work in my gallery. I have lots of friends in the industry and I'm sure a talent like yours will be well sought after. Looking forward to hearing from you.

> *Kind regards,*
> *Dolores x."*

A Year Later

The maître d' arrived at the table followed by Rafe, who was wearing a metallic pink shirt and a faded gray suit. He smiled at Pierce, who was sitting at the table, looking at his phone. When he sensed Rafe bending down and placing his head on Pierce's shoulder, Pierce put his cell down and jerked his head to kiss his boyfriend.

"Hi, baby," Rafe said and took a seat across Pierce, only separated by a tea light in a red jar. "How are you?"

Pierce took in the sight of his partner and sucked in a deep breath; he was truly breathtaking. He'd let his hair grow slightly, although he still had no traces of a beard, and any little he did have, he shaved daily. He took his jacket off, and his shirt tightened under the pressure of his protruding muscles. In all honesty, Pierce admired Rafe. Not only was he hard-working and committed, a great lover and boyfriend, but also looked after his health and body with immense results. And Pierce couldn't be prouder of how he'd turned out to be.

"I'm good," Pierce replied. "I was on the phone with Tracy earlier today, and she told me that the fundraising is going so well, she thinks we will be able to open the shelter earlier than we thought," Pierce went on and let his lips form the smile they'd been holding in.

Rafe tapped his hand on the table several times and bounced on his chair. "That's so exciting. And any news from Dolores?"

Pierce let himself be affected by the child-like glee that Rafe exhumed. "I did, indeed. She called me in the afternoon like she said she would. Apparently everyone loved the exhibition in Paris, and a few more art and photography curators have contacted her about doing more in London, Milan, Zurich, and surprisingly so, Moscow. She said she'll get the dates and let me know," he explained.

"Did you tell her you can't do August?"

Rafe nodded.

Pierce gasped. "What's in August?"

Rafe kicked him under the table.

"Oh, yeah, vacation time with my boyfriend in Maldives celebrating his twenty-first, how could I forget?"

Rafe frowned. "You better have not. It's the only time I managed to get off work, mister."

Pierce laughed. The waiter arrived at their table, and Pierce ordered non-alcoholic beer for both of them. When he left, he turned his full attention back to Rafe. "How was your work today, sweetie?"

"It was good. Got Marissa in the back today, started training her in all the office stuff. That girl's math is on fire. Even I struggled with some of the finance in my training. She swung it," he admitted.

"That's great." Pierce smiled and saw the waiter return with their drinks. "I knew she could do it. From the first day you hired her in The Tangerine as a waitress, she was a natural. Actually, considering her friend has managed to become a head manager of his own restaurant in the matter of a year, I wouldn't be shocked if she stole your job in a few months," he chuckled.

Rafe sat back and shook his finger in front of Pierce. "Cariño, if she *does* get better than me, I'll just fire her and send her elsewhere.

Puh-lease!"

They both laughed.

"Are you ready to order?"

Life was good. For the both of them. While Pierce had found his passion for snapping photos of the New Yorkers no one ever saw or read about, and made it into a profitable, charitable business, Rafe had found his place serving people and running an actual, brick-and-mortar business. He couldn't complain. They made quite the couple. With Rafe only hiring homeless people in his own restaurant, Pierce exhibiting his photographs across the world and helping to raise funds for a homeless center with his page Dreamless in New York, they made a good team.

Neither one of them would have made it where they were today if it hadn't been for the other. They'd been through each other's lowest, helped each other when they were ready to give up, and now they were being present for their transformation into thriving adults with a bright future ahead of them. Pierce didn't care much about anything other than Rafe. He would give everything else up in a heartbeat, but Rafe was the only future he couldn't imagine himself without.

Pierce took Rafe's hand. The waiter had just left with their order, Rafe following him before bringing his eyes back on Pierce.

"I love you, you know that?" Pierce told him, staring into his eyes.

"Me too," Rafe responded without missing a beat.

The spurting sound of firework candles cut through the restaurant as the waiter approached the table with a heart-shaped cake, singing "Happy Birthday," harmonized by Rafe's voice.

Pierce smiled and let them finish the song. Most of the other patrons had turned to look at the flashy cake and the singing gays. The waiter put the cake down on the table in front of Pierce, and he blew out the candle. He didn't make a wish. He was twenty-two, but he had everything he could ever want. He had Rafe.

The diners closest to them clapped for the birthday boy. "I know you like the dessert first, so I thought I'd surprise you by having it before our meal," Rafe explained.

Pierce felt a pull in his heart. He didn't mind it. It was what having your heart stolen felt like. The waiter handed him a knife to cut the cake. The thing was, just like Rafe knew Pierce, he also knew Rafe very well. Just like he knew Rafe loved to paint in his spare time and to let off steam, he knew Rafe was going to surprise him with a cake. He took the candle out from the edge of the cake and cut a piece around the hole. He put the piece on Rafe's plate, then cut another one for himself. The waiter didn't leave. He stood watching.

Rafe started eating. Pierce didn't. He watched as Rafe chewed and went down for another bite. Their waiter was still watching. Pierce saw a few more of the waiters doing the same. Those fuckers were going to ruin everything.

Rafe's spoon met resistance and he persisted. Traces of silver reflected the candle light.

"What is this?" Rafe asked as he cleared around the silver to reveal a ring with a sapphire in the middle.

Pierce didn't answer. He pushed his chair back and went down on his left knee. Or should it have been his right knee? He didn't know if there was importance or significance in it. It was too late to change it. He'd only look foolish. He took the ring out of Rafe's hands and held it in front of him, cake and all. Rafe stared at Pierce, his mouth agape and his hands frozen on top of the chocolate cake.

"Rafe, baby, you are my world," Pierce began. Damn, he hadn't even rehearsed it.

Rafe grabbed Pierce's hand. "What are you doing?" he looked around. Pierce didn't. He could tell everyone was watching. As if he needed more audience to stress him.

"From the moment I punched you, that October day, you changed my life." People laughed. The waiter laughed. Rafe laughed. "You gave it purpose and meaning. I-I was lost before you. Truly lost. But meeting you, becoming your friend, your lover, I learned more about the world than I could have without you. I learned so much about myself. You taught me how to be happy. And even though you might still call me a brute sometimes, I am happy. Only next to you did I even learn the meaning of the word. And next to you I found out what it is to love and be loved. I—know we'll be together for the rest of our lives and that we don't need a ring or a paper to make this any more real than it already is, but somehow this feels right." Pierce swallowed.

Rafe rolled his eyes. "Oh, say the truth, you just want everyone to know I'm taken." It seemed like the whole restaurant laughed.

Pierce did. "That too, but I want the world to know I'm yours also. So, will you agree to marry me, you thieving *cabron*?"

Rafe rubbed Pierce's cheek with his thumb, his eyes fixed on his. "It's *cabrón*, baby, not cabron. And of course I will marry, you fool."

Everything else blurred. The applause, the cheers, the whistles. That moment, it was just the two of them. Like it had always been.

Like it would always be. The brute and

the thief and a life happy together.

THE END

ACKNOWLEDGMENTS

I couldn't have written this book without some of the amazing people in my life.

First, and foremost, I would like to thank my Alphas, who have helped shaped the story before it was even put on paper. Natalie, Marco, MC, Jo and Alina; you have been great and instrumental in the creation of this book.

Secondly, I'd like to thank my editor, Kameron, for not allowing me to embarrass myself with my stray thoughts and poor punctuation skills.

Thirdly, I'd like to thank Rosa and Meredith for putting a name and a personality on Vance and making him who he is.

My deepest gratitude and love to Christina, who has always been there for me, listening to my constant moaning and writer problems and offering me her critical eye on anything from cover to story. Love you to bits.

I would like to thank Alex, for being himself and for helping me be mine. Thank you for your support in what I do. A million days, baby.

Last, but not least, I would like to thank you, the readers. Thank you for giving me your time by reading Pierce's and Rafe's story. Without you, I wouldn't be doing what I love. Telling the stories that are gnawing inside me.

Chris Ethan is a book whore. He enjoys selling his feelings for money and other pleasures and is blatantly unashamed to do so for as long as he breathes. Chris Ethan is also a persona for Rhys Christopher Ethan, author of fantasy and sci-fi. He uses Chris Ethan to share stories of adult queer romances with those who need it. Before you delve into his books however, be warned. He likes putting his characters through shitstorms and hates anything conventional. But then there's that darned happy-ever-after. Also, he likes swearing. Deal with it!

Visit rcethan.com/chris to follow
Chris' work and keep up with his news.

71376116R00190

Made in the USA
Columbia, SC
26 May 2017